WS

Please return/renew this item by the last date shown

worcestershire
countycouncil
Libraries & Learning

D0274933

Chinese Myths

Chinese Myths

SUN XUEGANG and CAI GUOYUN

Edited by
MEI LAN FRAME

Illustrated by
LEUYEN PHAM

VIKING
an imprint of
PENGUIN BOOKS

Published by the Penguin Group
Penguin Group (Australia)
250 Camberwell Road, Camberwell, Victoria 3124, Australia
(a division of Pearson Australia Group Pty Ltd)
Penguin Group (USA) Inc.
375 Hudson Street, New York, New York 10014, USA
Penguin Group (Canada)
90 Eglinton Avenue East, Suite 700, Toronto, Canada ON M4P 2Y3
(a division of Pearson Penguin Canada Inc.)
Penguin Books Ltd
80 Strand, London WC2R 0RL England
Penguin Ireland
25 St Stephen's Green, Dublin 2, Ireland
(a division of Penguin Books Ltd)
Penguin Books India Pvt Ltd
11 Community Centre, Panchsheel Park, New Delhi – 110 017, India
Penguin Group (NZ)
67 Apollo Drive, Rosedale, North Shore 0632, New Zealand
(a division of Pearson New Zealand Ltd)
Penguin Books (South Africa) (Pty) Ltd
24 Sturdee Avenue, Rosebank, Johannesburg 2196, South Africa

Penguin Books Ltd, Registered Offices: 80 Strand, London, WC2R 0RL, England

First published in China as *zhongguo shenhua* by China Children Publishing House, 2005
This English edition published by Penguin Group (Australia), 2008

1 3 5 7 9 10 8 6 4 2

Chinese Mythology original copyright © China Children Publishing House, 2005
English edition © Penguin Group (Australia), 2008
Illustrations copyright © LeUyen Pham, 2008
Edited by Mei Lan Frame

The moral right of the authors and illustrator has been asserted.

Design by Cathy Larsen © Penguin Group (Australia)
Illustrations by LeUyen Pham
Decorative elements are traditional Chinese designs courtesy of Dover Books
Typeset in 11/20pt Sabon by Post Pre-Press Group, Brisbane, Queensland
Printed in Australia by McPherson's Printing Group, Maryborough, Victoria

National Library of Australia
Cataloguing-in-Publication data:
Sun, Xuegang
Chinese myths / Sun Xuegang, Cai Guoyun; illustrator, LeUyen Pham.

ISBN: 978 0 670 07261 3.

398.20951

puffin.com.au

 This book was published with the support of a grant from SCIO China Book International.

Zhongguo Shenhua

SUN XUEGANG and CAI GUOYUN

Contents

Introduction

This collection of myths spans thousands of years of Chinese history – hundreds of thousands, even – passed down through the ages in both spoken and written form. It begins with a tale about the creation of the world by the giant Pan Gu, and ends with a story about a real-life kung fu master named Dong Haichuan. The myths in between tell us about incredible gods, goddesses and giants, all of whom once roamed the earth, at a time when the distance between heaven and earth was not so great. There are also legendary heroes and heroines, some of them gods and some merely human, but all remembered for their extraordinary feats of bravery and sacrifice.

Long ago, as with many myths around the world, the newly formed earth was plagued by many natural disasters. Because mankind was so young, it was up to gods and goddesses to save the earth. In 'How Gun Stole Xirang to Stop the Floods', you'll read about the terrible floods that threatened to destroy mankind. 'Archer Yi and the Ten Suns' describes an extreme heat wave that almost set the world ablaze. 'Gong Gong and the Collapse of Buzhou Mountain' tells of a rebel god called Gong Gong who caused the sun, moon and stars to orbit around the earth.

Chinese history also contains many legendary emperors and gods who were important in the creation of Chinese culture and science. Fu Xi is half god and half man, and because of his special birth he is able to climb up to heaven on a magical tree. There he finds plants and inventions and brings them down to earth as gifts for man. In 'Shao Hao and the Kingdom of Birds', Shao Hao assigns government roles to various types of birds so they may rule over his island. Later, the Bird Kingdom becomes the model for Chinese government on earth. The god Shennong leaves heaven to teach mankind about farming and irrigation, creating the first agricultural society. Later, he uses his understanding of nature to develop herbal Chinese medicine.

But gods are not the only focus of these myths; many of these stories are about real-life heroes and heroines who accomplished extraordinary feats. 'Mulan' is a famous story about a girl who becomes a fearless general in the Chinese army. 'Mazu, the Goddess of the Sea' explains how a girl with psychic powers rescues sailors from stormy seas. Still today, travellers in China can find monuments and temples in honour of both girls. 'Gao Liang and the Dragon King' is a story about a general who must bring back water to a parched and dry Beijing. The places mentioned in this story still exist today. If you're curious, find a city map of Beijing and look for an area called *Xi Zhi Men*, or the Western Gate; then you'll know exactly where Gao Liang pursued the Dragon King and Queen.

These Chinese myths are full of adventure and excitement, as well as being an absorbing mix of fact and fiction. I hope that in reading this collection you will enjoy a historical adventure through one of the world's oldest and largest civilisations. Look out for the companion volume to this collection, *Chinese Fairytales*. Together they provide a fascinating portrait of China and its history.

My thanks to all who helped me in working on this project, especially those at Penguin Australia and Penguin China, and my mother, for her help with translations. I would also like to thank Rishi Valley School in India, for providing me with the perfect fairytale cottage at the edge of a beautiful forest to write in.

Mei Lan Frame

Pan Gu and the Creation of Heaven and Earth

Long, long ago, before there was heaven and earth, the universe was in complete darkness and silence. The only thing that existed was the universe itself, shaped like a huge egg, in which there was neither light nor sound.

After a long time, a baby appeared in this egg. No one knows how or why. The baby grew and grew, feeding off the emptiness inside the universe. He was asleep and kept his eyes tightly shut. His body never moved but remained crouched inside the egg. At last, after eighteen thousand years of sleep, the baby woke up.

First, the baby opened his eyes, but he saw nothing, for there was nothing but darkness. Then he wanted to move his body, but he couldn't, for there was no room. Finally, he let out a cry and, with an enormous effort, stretched his body. There was a huge splitting noise as the egg around the baby cracked and shafts of light escaped from inside. The universe was no longer dark or silent, and Pan Gu, the creator of the universe, was born.

The sound of creation continued, and all that was *Yang* (light and pure) floated upward to become heaven, and all that was *Yin* (heavy and mixed) fell downwards to become earth. Pan Gu reached up with his arms to support heaven while his feet pressed firmly on earth.

Pan Gu grew and grew in the space between heaven and earth, and the distance between them became greater. After each day, Pan Gu had grown one *zhang* (a little over three metres) and heaven became one *zhang* higher. As a result, the heavier particles fell downwards, making earth one *zhang* thicker.

Then Pan Gu breathed the air between heaven and earth and he began to speak. His eyes became bright as they took in the splendour of creation. By now he had teeth in his mouth, and hair on his head, and a moustache and beard on his face. Water streamed down his body and this became his flowing blood. It poured over the stones and rocks that formed his muscles. Pan Gu had become a god.

He looked up at heaven and down at earth, and he knew he had unlimited strength. He could remain standing there between heaven and earth forever.

After another eighteen thousand years, heaven had reached its highest point and it was impossible for earth to be any thicker. By then, the gap between them had grown to ninety thousand *li* (around forty-five thousand kilometres), and Pan Gu was gigantic. With his enormous strides, he ran great distances over the earth. His shouts bellowed throughout the lands and sometimes he heard echoes of his voice from distances far away.

Yet as Pan Gu travelled over the newly formed world, he found places where heaven and earth were not completely separated. He worried that the two would rejoin and extinguish light and sound, destroying all the work he had done. Then one day he found two shining objects, a chisel and an axe. He knew that Tian Di, the Supreme God, had placed them there for him to use. Pan Gu picked up the chisel with his left hand and the axe with his right, and began the task of completing the separation of heaven and earth.

Every time Pan Gu struck the chisel with the axe, the sounds reverberated throughout the world. The universe grew in size, and the light between heaven and earth shone brighter. Pan Gu worked tirelessly day and night, and finally there were no places left where heaven and earth were still connected.

Pan Gu was delighted when he saw that his task was finished, and he let out an enormous cry of joy. At that same moment, he suddenly felt extremely tired and could no longer stand up. He knew that because he had fulfilled his task, it was time to rest. Slowly, he lay down and closed his eyes. His breathing became peaceful and then stopped. Pan Gu never woke up again.

With his death, Pan Gu gave to the universe a wonderful inheritance. His last breath became the wind and the clouds, while the sound of his breathing became thunder. After his death, his left eye became the sun, and his right eye the moon. His body became the five sacred mountains, his arms and legs the four directions, north, south, east and west, of earth. The blood that flowed in his body became water for the rivers and oceans, while his veins became their routes. His muscles turned into soil, and the hair on his head formed the stars in the sky. His skin and the soft hairs that covered it grew into flowers, grass and trees, while his bones and teeth became metal and minerals. The energy in his body and the marrow in his bones crystallized into gems and jade, and the sweat that once cooled him became rain.

Pan Gu separated heaven and earth and made the universe as we know it. His story represents both nature and mankind, symbolising our love for the world and our ability to create.

Nu Wa, the Mother of Mankind

After Pan Gu's death, the sun, moon and stars shone brightly over the earth. Over the mountains and the plains, lush forests and grasslands flourished, fed by glistening rivers and rain. At that time, the space between heaven and earth was filled with heavy particles, and these particles floated into the waters and land and were absorbed, creating new life.

After tens of thousands of years, animals came into being. Birds flew in the sky, fish swam in the seas and large animals ran in the forests. The variety of creatures covered the world with their sounds and songs, and from then on the earth and the sky were never silent.

During this time, a beautiful and powerful goddess by the name of Nu Wa was born. She was the caretaker of the new world and wandered between heaven and earth, making sure that the sun, moon and stars followed their rhythms, and that nature provided all that was needed. Nu Wa was happy as she wandered alone throughout creation, yet after a while she began to feel lonely, because neither the trees and flowers, nor the birds, beasts and fish were the same as she. They looked different and spoke to each other in languages that Nu Wa couldn't understand.

One day, Nu Wa came to a riverbank and decided to rest. The river flowed silently and smoothly, and Nu Wa saw her reflection in the clear water. She began to comb her long hair, wondering all the time why there were no other creatures like her, even after so many generations of life. 'If there were,' she thought, 'then wouldn't the world be a wonderful place!'

With this in mind, Nu Wa picked up a clump of wet clay from the riverbank. Then she concentrated all her thoughts on shaping a small creature that looked like her. When she had finished, she placed the clay figure of a baby on the ground. It absorbed the energy of the earth and began to move, stretching out its arms. 'Ma! Ma!' the baby cried and ran towards Nu Wa. Delighted, she bent down to pick it up and cradled it in her arms.

The baby soon grew into a creature just like Nu Wa. She called this creature 'man', and as she looked at the first man she created Nu Wa felt very satisfied. She decided to shape more babies from clay. Soon, there were lots of babies, and they gathered around Nu Wa and called her 'Mother'. Nu Wa no longer felt lonely because of her many children.

Nu Wa worked day and night to keep creating babies. It was exhausting work, and she would often have to stop and rest. When her babies grew up, they left her and went to every corner of the world. Yet the world was so large that Nu Wa thought it would be impossible for her to

fill it with men, especially if she had to shape every baby from clay.

Then Nu Wa had an idea. She found a hollow reed of bamboo and stuck the tip of the reed into the wet clay. The reed filled with clay, and Nu Wa swung it towards the ground, dotting the earth with little lumps of clay. Magically, these little batches of clay formed into babies exactly like the ones she had been creating. The goddess Nu Wa was extremely happy and began to create more babies with her bamboo reed.

After a while, the earth was filled with men, and Nu Wa decided to rest. She looked joyfully at the many men she had created, pleased with how her creations lived together on the earth. But then Nu Wa noticed that the first men she had created were getting old, and she started to worry that they would soon die and she would have to create more men. How was it possible for man to continue without her?

Nu Wa pondered this question day and night, until finally she saw how nature had created animals that were both male and female. She realised that humans could also be made into males and females, and therefore be able to have children and continue as a family. So she gathered all her offspring together and divided them into men and women, telling them to marry and have children. She prayed to heaven, asking the gods to work as divine matchmakers for men and women. After that, human beings began to have their own children, and Nu Wa's task was of creating babies was fulfilled.

Nu Wa Restores the Sky

After the creation of human beings, the earth became filled with people. Nu Wa returned to heaven to act as the divine matchmaker for men and women. Soon there were many families and, because human beings were clever and inventive, their lives became better and more peaceful. Nu Wa was pleased to see their fortunes increasing, and she was happy that people had settled in all four corners of the earth.

Then suddenly, a terrible thing happened. In the sky

above them, people on earth heard a tremendous crash, like the sound of a thousand booming rolls of thunder, and huge pieces of rock and stone began to rain down. Looking up, they saw a big black hole in the sky. Out of the hole came burning rocks of fire, which set the trees and the mountains alight. These rocks made deep craters in the land and caused water to gush up from underground rivers, flooding the valleys and lowlands where people lived.

Everyone ran in terror from the catastrophes around them. The sky continued to rain down fire and stone, and floods ruined the farmlands and houses people had built. They had no choice but to hide in caves for shelter. Meanwhile, dangerous beasts abandoned their homes in the forest in search of food. Tigers, dragons, snakes and eagles began to attack human beings. 'Please help us!' the people cried out to heaven. 'Save us from these disasters!'

Nu Wa heard their cries up in heaven and rushed down to the human world. There, she saw the earth in chaos, while her people suffered and died. Looking for the cause of the disasters, Nu Wa discovered the enormous hole in the sky. 'How terrible!' she thought. 'Humans will never be able to fix this and shall surely perish. I will have to save my people by fixing the hole myself.'

She went to a big river and collected as many precious gems as she could find. She gathered sapphires, diamonds, rubies and emeralds, and these gems shone with the same colours and depth as the sky. After placing them together in a giant pot, Nu Wa made a fire on the riverbank and set the pot to boil. She had to tend the fire for several days before the gems melted. Finally, her mixture became a shiny, sticky glue of many colours. Though she was tired, Nu Wa then made a long spade. She used the spade to patch the sky with her colourful glue. After a long time, the glue of melted gems mixed in with the sky, and the sky was restored, shining as brightly as it had before.

Once the hole in the sky was fixed, the fires in the forests and mountains died down, and Nu Wa filled up the deep craters to stop the gushing water. But the surface

of the sky was still fragile, and Nu Wa was worried that another hole might appear again one day. She needed to find a way to support the sky. So she went down to the sea and caught a magic sea turtle and used its four limbs as columns. The turtle was so huge that its limbs reached the four corners of the world. In this way, the sky became stable and would never collapse again.

Yet the land was still covered in water, and people were unable to return to their homes. Worse still, there was an evil black dragon that roamed the waters, and he had already eaten many people and animals. The dragon was skilled in black magic, and he used his power to raise the wicked spirits of the floods to terrorise people. Lakes and seas became filled with snakes and other dangerous creatures. Nu Wa knew that her people were no match for the black dragon, and again she vowed to help them.

First, Nu Wa had to make the water recede. She went to the river and plucked as many reeds as she could carry from the riverbank. Then she made a giant fire and placed the reeds on top of it. They quickly burned to ashes, and Nu Wa scooped up the ashes and deposited them all over the land, making more hills and mountains. As a result, the water had no choice but to flow into the sea and its force drove all the snakes and creatures back into the woods. The black dragon, powerless now that he was on dry land, fled deep into the ocean. Frightened of Nu Wa's power, he never dared to bother humans again.

People were now free to return to their homes, and animals and beasts were also free to return to the forest. Soon life on the earth had become peaceful again. Now that the waters had receded, trees, flowers, grass and crops sprung up from the ground and everything prospered. People were grateful to Nu Wa and built temples to praise her and give thanks.

But Nu Wa hadn't helped mankind just to receive their praises, so she made a musical instrument called the Sheng Huang for them. She gave it to her people and taught them how to use it to make music and song. The people were thrilled with their gift, and they sang and danced for many days and nights without end.

In the midst of their celebration, Nu Wa silently left the human world in a thunder carriage carried by dragons. Surrounded by yellow clouds and led by gods, she reached the highest realm of heaven and saw the Supreme God, Tian Di. From that day on she lived in heaven, but she never boasted or talked about her achievements. In her eyes, she had only followed the laws of heaven and done what she should have done.

Gong Gong and the Collapse of Buzhou Mountain

Many years after the creation of the earth, the universe came under the control of a god named Zhuan Xu. Before his rule, heaven and earth lived in peace and harmony, but once Zhuan Xu took over, everything changed. Zhuan Xu was a terrible ruler who wanted to control everything. He did whatever he pleased, and the gods who opposed him were punished and banished from heaven. Soon there was no one left to challenge Zhuan Xu, and disasters started happening in the human world.

One day, Zhuan Xu decided to test his strength. He fixed the position of the sun, the moon and all the stars in the northern sky so that they no longer moved. As a result, life on earth became very strange. Where there was sun in the north, people lived under constant daylight and couldn't sleep. Their crops grew too quickly and wilted in the heat. Their animals became restless and soon ran away. As for the people in the south, they lived in constant darkness. No crops, plants or flowers could grow because of the lack of light.

Zhuan Xu let the people suffer to show his authority and force them to bow down to him. He demanded sacrifices and continual worship. Then he boasted to the other gods, saying that he was stronger and mightier than any of them.

But there was one god in heaven who could not stand Zhuan Xu's rule any longer. His name was Gong Gong, and he was the God of Water. One day he summoned the other gods together. 'I can't take any more of Zhuan Xu's overbearing ways! How long do we have to tolerate his rule?'

The other gods were also unhappy, but because they had been bullied by Zhuan Xu for so long, they did not know what to do. Yet Gong Gong would not give up. 'Zhuan Xu has failed in his task to look after the universe, so we should join together and force him out of his position as Supreme God.'

All the gods quickly agreed. 'Yes!' they shouted. 'If we join together, we can overthrow Zhuan Xu and restore peace and harmony.'

Gong Gong asked the other gods to prepare an army. Then, leading the army of gods and soldiers, Gong Gong went to find Zhuan Xu to declare war.

When Zhuan Xu heard that Gong Gong was declaring war, he was shocked. He would never have believed the other gods would join together to challenge him. But he was confident of his own power, and he marched out with his massive army to meet Gong Gong on the battlefield.

At the battlefield, the two armies stood facing one another. Zhuan Xu was the first to speak. 'Gong Gong,' he shouted, 'how dare you lead this rebellion against me? Let's see how I will punish you!'

But Gong Gong was not afraid. Pointing his spear at Zhuan Xu, he said, 'You have dislodged the sun, the moon and the stars from their rightful paths. You have banished all the gods who oppose you. You are not fit to be Supreme God of the Universe. We will fight to overthrow you!' With this, Gong Gong let out a cry and charged towards Zhuan Xu.

A huge battle began. Throughout both heaven and earth, soldiers and gods fought against one another, and their cries of war were heard across the land. In the sunlit north, the warring armies shattered cliffs and rocks, and great clouds of dust rose up. In the darkness of the north, they fought by torchlight and fire, and the land was under constant threat from the flames.

As the battle wore on, neither side was able to gain the upper hand. The two armies were perfectly matched in skill and size. Finally, they fought all the way to Buzhou Mountain in the southeast.

Buzhou Mountain was so tall that its peak was hidden in the clouds, and it was so steep that no trees, flowers or grass grew there. It was one of the columns that supported the sky, and it marked the end of the earth.

Gong Gong's army continued to fight at the foot of Buzhou Mountain, but they could not get an advantage.

Gong Gong started to worry. He was leading a rebellion against Zhuan Xu, and his army had not yet won a single battle. His promise to overthrow Zhuan Xu seemed impossible. But Gong Gong was a stubborn and strong-willed god and would not admit defeat. He grew angrier and angrier, until one day he looked up at Buzhou Mountain and shouted, 'You column of heaven, why are you so unfair? Why don't you let me defeat Zhuan Xu?'

In a fit of rage, he charged towards the mountain and crashed into it. There was a deafening noise that sent vibrations throughout the land. The ground trembled as a massive crack appeared in the middle of the mountain and then it collapsed to the ground.

Both armies saw that the column of heaven had been

shattered and ran away in fear. Great changes were already taking place on the earth. Without the support of Buzhou Mountain in the south, the sky tilted upwards in the north. This caused the sun, the moon and stars that Zhuan Xu had fixed in place to start sliding to the west. Some moved faster and some moved slower, all from east to west, following their respective paths. As they gathered momentum, they began to orbit around the earth. Wherever the sun went, the earth was covered in daylight. When the sun departed to shine on another part of the earth, it became night. People, animals and plants were never tortured by everlasting day or night again.

When Buzhou Mountain came crashing to the ground, a gigantic pit was created. The once-level land now tilted to the southeast. All the rivers and lakes went gushing towards the pit, gradually filling it with water. Soon, the pit had become the South China Sea.

Seeing all the changes that had occurred, Zhuan Xu was terrified. He thought that Gong Gong had gathered all of nature to fight against him, and ran away in fear. Throughout the entire universe, no one heard from him again.

As for Gong Gong, he regretted charging into Buzhou Mountain and bringing down a column of heaven. Fearing that Tian Di would punish him, he quickly fled as well, taking refuge in the South China Sea.

Although Gong Gong did not defeat Zhuan Xu in battle, his collision with Buzhou Mountain created the orbit of the sun, moon and stars, and the flow of the rivers into the sea. Because of this contribution to the earth, people everywhere praised him.

Fu Xi, the Son of God and Man

Long ago, during the ancient times of history, there was a kingdom in the northwest of China known as Huaxu. This kingdom was known throughout the lands as a paradise. The people of Huaxu lived until they were hundreds of years old, and they were never troubled by floods or fire. Many claimed the people of Huaxu even had the ability to fly up into the sky.

One girl who lived in this kingdom was called Huaxu Shi. She led a happy, carefree life and often spent her days wandering outdoors. One day, she was playing near a swamp. The swamp was called 'Lei Zi', for it belonged to the God of Thunder. It was an enchanting spot, surrounded by lush green trees and high grass that shimmered in the wind. Walking along the border of the swamp, Huaxu Shi came upon a footprint pressed deep into the earth that was unlike anything she had even seen. It was easily as tall as a grown man and looked like the footprint of both a man and a dragon. 'Whose footprint is this? It's so big!' Huaxu Shi said to herself. Curious, she stepped inside.

The big footprint belonged to the God of Thunder. He had the head and body of a man, but the wings and claws of a dragon. He was a powerful god, in charge of creating thunder by banging a drum. When he was tired, he often went to his swamp to rest. He left huge footprints in the earth wherever he walked that were full of his magical power and energy.

Now, Hauxu Shi did not know that she was stepping into the footprint of a god. As soon as her foot touched the imprinted earth, her stomach growled and she felt a little faint. Deciding to return home, Huaxu Shi climbed out of the footprint and began the journey back. By the time she had reached her house, her belly was swollen and she knew that she was pregnant.

Before long, Huaxu Shi gave birth to a boy, whom she called Fu Xi. Because his father was the God of Thunder, Fu Xi was half man and half god. From the time Fu Xi was a small child, his mother realised he had the personality of a human, but the talent and strength of a god.

As he grew up, Fu Xi was able to do many things that ordinary men couldn't do. One day, he heard about a magical tree called Jianmu. This tree was also known as the heavenly ladder, because it connected the human world to heaven. Jianmu stood tall and straight, reaching all the way to the clouds. It never cast a shadow, even when the sun was directly behind it, and it never swayed, no matter how strongly the winds blew. Yet its trunk was so soft that anyone who tried to climb it quickly fell to the ground, for the tree would bend as easily as a tassel on a hat. No man on earth had ever climbed it before.

Fu Xi decided he would climb the magical tree. He left the kingdom of Huaxu and journeyed to the south, until he reached the sacred forest. There, he climbed the tallest tree he could find, and scanned the forest for Jianmu. But he could see no other treetops taller than the one he was in. Looking up, Fu Xi noticed that the top of his tree reached all the way into the clouds. He had already found the heavenly ladder! Fu Xi continued to climb, even higher than the clouds, until he finally arrived at the gate of heaven.

In heaven, Fu Xi learned the ways of the gods. Through meditation and study, Fu Xi gained more and more knowledge. Yet because Fu Xi was half human, he did not wish to stay in heaven, for he missed the earth below. He also remembered how difficult life was for humans, and he was determined to use his new knowledge to help people live a better life. From then on, Fu Xi only journeyed up to heaven to bring knowledge back to earth.

One invention Fu Xi brought back was a fishing net, which he made by following the pattern of a spider web.

Fu Xi had watched how spiders on earth spun a web to catch their prey, and he noticed that the web managed to hold whatever was caught. But when he tried to make a net on earth, he found that neither the thread that people used for cloth nor the bark from trees was strong enough. He travelled up to heaven and discovered a plant called hemp that had tough fibres. Using this plant, he was able to make strong ropes and then fashion the ropes into a fishing net.

Back on earth, Fu Xi gave the net to the people and showed them how to use it. Soon, they were catching more fish than ever before. Then Fu Xi showed them how to make a fire so they wouldn't have to eat their food raw. He went into the forest and found a small fire burning on a tree where it had been struck by lightning. He brought the burning branch back to the people and made a huge bonfire. The people were delighted and prepared a delicious feast of cooked fish for him.

With the improvements in people's lives, they began to build small houses along riverbanks and lakes. They

started trading food and other goods, but they had no method of keeping track of what they bought or sold. Fu Xi went up to heaven again, and brought back more ropes from the hemp plant. He showed people how to make knots in the rope and taught them how to add and subtract. Each knot in the rope stood for a number, and people were able to keep track of their goods and make simple calculations.

Soon people began to use maths in their daily lives and their curiosity grew. To give people a deeper understanding of numbers, Fu Xi taught them the formula for the Magic Square. The Magic Square is made up of nine numbers in three rows, like a square. When these rows are added, they always equal the same number. People were fascinated by the puzzle of the Magic Square, and their knowledge of numbers and mathematics grew and grew.

But Fu Xi was still not satisfied with all that he had done. He noticed that people's lives were often threatened by danger and natural disasters. So he returned to heaven yet again to gain the knowledge of the Eight Diagrams. The Eight Diagrams took into account the two forces of the universe, Yin and Yang, and showed all the possible changes that could happen in the world. With the knowledge of the Eight Diagrams, people were able to make predictions about the future and their lives became much more secure.

Finally, Fu Xi sat down and looked at all the knowledge he had given to men. He saw that people's lives were easier and they were busy with work, and he was pleased. Yet he also noticed that when people rested, they had little to do and would soon become bored. So on Fu Xi's last trip up the heavenly ladder, he returned with music and musical instruments. He taught the people how to play simple tunes that he had heard in heaven. Then he showed them how to dance to the music. Now people had a meaningful way to rest, as well as a way to enjoy themselves. With the start of dancing and music, Chinese culture began to develop.

The people were grateful for all that Fu Xi had done

for them, so when he died, they appealed to heaven to make him the Supreme God of the East. Heaven granted their wish, and Fu Xi was given a place as an immortal among the gods. Even today, if you visit a temple in China, you can find altars for Fu Xi. He is regarded as the creator of civilisation and an example of all that people can achieve.

Shennong and the Treasure Rice

In the early years of mankind, when people still hunted for food, there lived a legendary emperor by the name of Shennong. Shennong had the body of a man, but the head of a bull. Together with Zhu Rong, the God of Fire, he ruled the southern sky in the heavens. One day, after seeing how quickly the population on earth was growing, he decided to leave heaven and teach people how to farm.

Shennong knew that people could not live by hunting animals forever. In the colder months, when game became scarce, people often fell ill or even starved. And many animals had been driven out of their forest homes by groups of hunters. So, before he descended from heaven, Shennong took with him five types of seeds. These were rice, millet, wheat, beans and hemp.

When Shennong came to earth, nine deep wells appeared at his feet, and from their depths bubbled forth clear spring water that overflowed onto the ground. Shennong used his bamboo cane to dig lots of small holes in the ground, and the water soaked down to the arid soil below. Plants and flowers in the once-dry soil now sprang to life, and from this people learned the method of irrigation.

Next Shennong summoned a crowd of people together and took out the five types of seeds from his pouch. He told the people to remove all the rocks and stones in the soil and then to plow the earth in rows. Shennong placed the seeds in the earth and covered them over with soil. After a few days, seedlings appeared in the ground. He showed the people how to irrigate and fertilise the crops and pull up the harmful weeds. By autumn, the seedlings had grown, and Shennong returned to teach people how to harvest their crops. These crops were delicious and easier to digest than the meat of beasts and birds. The people were delighted and began farming, as well as hunting and fishing, for their food.

One day, a red bird flew high over the field, carrying some corn in its beak. As it flew, the golden kernels fell onto the ground by the farmers' feet. Believing that the kernels were a gift from heaven, the people ran to find Shennong. 'This is corn,' he told them, and advised them to plant the kernels in the ground. After a while, tall stalks with huge ears of ripe corn covered the field, and the people were overjoyed with their crop. They named the grain 'treasure rice', for it was unlike anything they had seen before.

That winter, after the harvest season, the farmers held a festival to show their gratitude to Shennong. They made a delicious feast with the grain they had stored, and celebrated with songs and dance. However, Shennong's mind

was preoccupied, and he wanted to be alone to think. So he silently left the festival and headed towards the mountains of Xianyang.

Shennong was thinking about the many illnesses that people suffered. He had watched as patients became sick and sometimes even died because no one knew how to cure their diseases. He wondered if some of the plants in the mountains could be used as medicine to heal the sick.

When he reached the mountains, he found all types of plants. But how could he tell if the plants would cure disease? He sat and meditated on the secrets of nature for many days and nights in the forest without food or water. When he awoke from his trance, he understood the principles of medicine according to Yin and Yang and the Five Elements. He could now understand the nature of diseases and how they affected people.

Using the leaves of a sacred plant, Shennong made a magical whip to help him. After he lashed at a plant with his whip, he would touch the plant to feel if it was warm, cold or hot. In this way, Shennong could tell what medicine the plant would make, and whether it was poisonous or safe to use.

Shennong knew he would have to try all the plants himself to test them as medicine. He chewed the leaves and noticed their flavour; some were sweet while others were very bitter. During his meditation, Shennong's skin became transparent, and he was able to see inside his body to his internal organs. Whenever he ate a herb or a leaf, he would watch to see where it went in his body and what diseases it could cure.

Once, Shennong ate a poisonous herb by mistake. He immediately fainted and fell to the ground. Luckily, thanks to his divine spirit, he soon woke up. He looked at his body to see what damage the poison had done, and this enabled him to create a cure. After that, Shennong experimented with many poisonous herbs so that he could create the antidotes.

After trying hundreds of herbs, Shennong discovered the cures for all kinds of diseases. He collected the leaves from different plants and dried them in the sun, then pounded them into powders. With the powders, he mixed various ingredients together and then rolled them into pills. When they were ready, he came down from the mountain and distributed the medicines to the people.

Those who were suffering from illness or disease soon regained their health. They praised Shennong, saying, 'These medicines must surely be from heaven!'

But Shennong explained to them, 'I found these plants in the mountains. There is no need for you to look to heaven for medicine.'

The people were overjoyed to learn that medicine could be found on earth. 'Please teach us your knowledge,' they said. So, after gathering a group of young students to join him, Shennong set off once again to the mountains.

Shennong led his students through woods and valleys for many days, until finally they reached the peaks and cliffs where the plants grew. On seeing the colourful and fragrant herbs, some students wanted to taste them. But Shennong warned them about trying unknown plants.

'Testing medicine is very dangerous!' he said. 'You are just ordinary men, and your bodies cannot handle the effects. If you find a new plant, let me know and I will test it for you.'

All his students agreed, and they travelled further into the mountains to deep forests that Shennong had not visited before.

Whenever a new plant was discovered, the students gave it to Shennong to try. By the end of the expedition, they had classified over one thousand different herbs, and knew their effects on the body. Along the way, they also discovered other plants such as peas, sorghum and soy. So, besides returning with medicine, they also brought back more crops for cultivation.

Realising that humans were now skilled in farming and medicine, Shennong retired from his role as emperor and moved to a place called Taiyuan. There, he continued his research and study of medicine. He spent many years in Taiyuan, and before he left to return to heaven he bestowed upon the people a cooking pot to prepare medicines. The people kept this pot for generations. Even today, it is still possible to visit the city of Taiyuan and see the ancient pot that Shennong used.

In heaven, Shennong became the God of Agriculture and Medicine for Chinese people. He symbolises the relationship between mankind and nature, and the profound effect that the two can have on each other.

Shao Hao and the Kingdom of Birds

Long ago, when the distance between the earth and heaven was only separated by the Milky Way, there lived a beautiful young fairy by the name of Huang E. She was a weaver in the imperial palace of heaven, and she spent her days at a loom weaving gossamer-thin cloth. Often she would work deep into the night, and her eyes would grow tired. At these times, she would get up from her loom and walk out of the palace to the banks of the Milky Way. Whenever she looked at the shimmering surface of the heavenly river, she always felt refreshed.

Sometimes, Huang E went sailing on the Milky Way in a small boat. She would row her boat upstream and disembark at the foot of a qiongsang tree. This tree was so tall that no one standing on the ground below could see all the way to the very top. Its leaves shone red like the setting sun, and its fruit was large and sweet. It was said that the fruit only ripened once every ten thousand years and whoever ate the ripe fruit would live forever. Huang E loved the tree and would often lie and watch its gently waving branches.

One night, Huang E was resting under the tree when she saw a young man walking towards her. The young man was very handsome and graceful. He also looked familiar. He watched Huang E for some time, and then came over to speak to her.

'I am the son of the White Emperor,' he said. 'Every morning I patrol the eastern sky and guide the sunrise.'

Huang E finally recognised him. 'So that's who you are!' she said, delighted. 'You are the bright morning and evening star, isn't that right?'

The young man nodded. 'Yes, they call me Venus. Before I begin my work every morning, I like to visit the Milky Way. I have often seen you here.'

Huang E was thrilled to meet Venus, and she invited him to play some music with her. Venus played a stringed instrument called the Se, and Huang E accompanied him with her singing. Their music echoed down the length of the Milky Way, making the stars in the river shine even more brightly. They continued to play music far into the night, and when the time came for his morning duties Venus was reluctant to leave. He asked Huang E to meet him again by the qiongsang tree.

From then on, Venus and Huang E often met under the tree. Sometimes, they would step in Huang E's small boat and Venus would row them upstream. They loved to watch the scenes on earth as they sailed on the Milky Way. One night, Huang E broke off a branch from a cherry tree and this became the mast of their boat. Venus picked some fragrant lavender and tied it to the mast as their banner. Then they made a compass out of jade and used it to guide them. Both Venus and Huang E were very happy, and Huang E decided never to return to the imperial palace. Instead, she and Venus lived together on their small boat, sailing up and down the Milky Way.

Soon, Huang E learned she was pregnant. She decided she should make a home on earth. Venus was very sad, for he knew he could not go with her. He had to continue his work in the heavens. The couple said a tearful goodbye, but promised they would be together again one day.

Before long, Huang E gave birth to a son. She called him Shao Hao and raised him according to the ways of earth. As he grew, he became a handsome young man, just like his father. One day, he asked Huang E about his father, for they had always lived alone.

'You are the son of the god Venus,' she told him. 'And I am the fairy Huang E, who once lived in the imperial palace of heaven.'

Shao Hao was astonished by his mother's words, for he had always thought of himself as an ordinary man.

'You are the offspring of two immortals,' she went on,

gently, 'so you should go to a distant place and create a new world. This will be your own kingdom.'

Shao Hao thought about his mother's advice. 'You are right,' he said finally. 'I will go to the eastern paradise, for this is where my father works.'

Shao Hao began his journey the next morning. He went to the East Sea and sailed on a boat until he reached a distant island. Stepping onto the island, he proclaimed himself the king. However, his kingdom differed from other kingdoms for there were no people on the island, only birds. Shao Hao had inherited his mother's love of nature and solitude, and decided he did not want to rule over a group of noisy, troublesome humans. The day after he arrived, he sent off a pigeon with the message that he had established a kingdom for birds. The message spread throughout the earth, and all kinds of birds flew to the island to become part of the new kingdom. Shao Hao was delighted by the arrival of the many birds, and he climbed upon his throne to watch as they flew to meet him.

The first to arrive was Phoenix, so following the order

of a royal court, Shao Hao appointed Phoenix as his prime minister and told him to take charge of the calendar. Then he asked Swallow, Butcherbird, Sparrow and Golden Pheasant to take charge of the four seasons. Pigeon was very conscientious, so Shao Hao appointed him as minister of education and asked him to take charge of schooling and ethics. Golden Eagle was strong and good at combat, so he was ordered to take care of military affairs and defense. Cuckoo was skilled at housekeeping, so he became responsible for building houses and waterways. The just and unselfish White Eagle took charge of criminal law, while Dove, because of his peaceful nature, handled cases of mediation. The cultivation and harvest in the fields were taken care of by the industrious and hard-working Swan. The other birds served as carpenters, metal smiths, potters, weavers and dyers.

Shao Hao assigned duties and responsibilities to all the birds. The birds looked up to Shao Hao with respect, grateful that he had established a kingdom for them on earth. They decided to call Shao Hao 'White Emperor',

since they knew that Shao Hao was the grandson of the White Emperor in heaven.

Yet the kingdom was not always peaceful. When Shao Hao summoned his ministers to court, they would often quarrel bitterly with one another. Sometimes the arguments turned into a fight, and feathers of different colours would fly around the court, creating a mess.

Finally, Shao Hao had had enough. He decided to change himself into a huge vulture whenever a meeting was called. As a vulture, he had a wingspan that was twice the size of the other birds, and he would watch them with a ferocious gleam in his eye. When he sat in the middle of the proceedings, none of the other birds dared to quarrel. In this way, Shao Hao restored order and peace to his court.

Shao Hao ruled over his kingdom in the East Sea for many, many years. The island became a flourishing paradise for birds, and later a model for government in human society. Even today, when people look at the sky over the East Sea, they often see numerous birds hovering at the edge of the horizon.

How Gun Stole Xirang to Stop the Floods

Long, long ago, during the ancient times on earth, the sky began to rain. It rained and rained for days without end, and rivers and lakes started to overflow their banks. The rain continued for several weeks, until all the houses and farmlands in China were under water. Even after several months the rains had not stopped, and the land became like a great, vast sea.

With nowhere left to live on the plains, the people moved into the hills. They tried to farm there, but the continual rain washed away all the seeds and crops. So they took to hunting, but most of the birds and animals had drowned in the flood and there was no food to be found.

Every creature on earth suffered greatly. The rain was relentless and it covered the land in turbulent, rushing waters. The people appealed to the gods for help, begging them to stop the flood, but their prayers went unanswered. For over twenty years it rained, and the earth became a place of great suffering and misery.

The gods saw what was happening on earth and felt great sympathy. One god by the name of Gun was especially moved by the destruction and sadness caused by the flood. He wanted to help those who were dying from hunger and cold. He decided to approach Tian Di, the Supreme God, to see if he would agree to use his magical powers to stop the rains and restore life on earth.

'Heavenly Emperor,' said Gun, as he knelt before Tian Di's throne, 'on behalf of all the gods, I ask you to stop this catastrophe on earth, for life is being destroyed.'

But Tian Di was unmoved by Gun's plea. 'I will not intervene,' he said, 'for such is the way of heaven and the way of nature. You are wrong to meddle in such affairs.'

Gun was greatly saddened as he left the imperial court. But he could not give up the idea of saving the human world. He looked at the submerged lands, wondering how to control the floods. For several days he kept silent, frowning at the destruction he saw.

Then one day while Gun was meditating, an owl and a turtle approached him, walking hand in hand. These were no normal animals; they were sacred and knew much about the ways of heaven. They saw that Gun was frowning and asked, 'Why are you so unhappy?'

'Because the floods are destroying people,' answered Gun, 'and I can't see any way to stop them.'

The owl looked at Gun thoughtfully. 'So you want to control the floods and save human beings?' he said. 'This could be difficult, and it could be easy.'

Gun was puzzled by the owl's response. 'Why is that?' he asked. 'Do you know of a method that would help me?'

The sacred turtle spoke up. 'We know of a magic soil called Xirang that multiplies by itself. When a handful of Xirang is thrown on the ground, more soil appears. If you use Xirang, then you can control the floods.'

Gun stopped frowning and stood up. 'Where is this Xirang?' he asked excitedly. 'Tell me and I will gather some right now.'

But the owl and the turtle only shook their heads. 'We've heard about it, but we don't know where you can find it.'

'No matter,' Gun said adamantly. 'If I look for it, I'm sure I will find it. Then I'll throw Xirang all over the earth to block the floods and save the human world.'

The owl's eyes widened in surprise. 'The Supreme God will never allow you to do that,' he warned. 'Aren't you afraid of his punishment?'

But Gun did not care about the consequences. So, bidding the owl and the turtle goodbye, he began to search heaven for Xirang. For several days he roamed everywhere, looking for the magic soil, until finally he stumbled upon a mysterious cave that went deep into the side of a mountain. Inside the cave was an altar to heaven, and on top of the altar was a large clay bowl filled with soil. Gun knew the soil was the magical Xirang.

But the clay bowl was guarded by two gods, so Gun had to wait for them to leave their post. Finally the gods were called away, and Gun stole the bowl of Xirang and immediately left heaven for the human world.

As he descended towards earth, Gun threw a handful of Xirang into the raging floodwaters below him. Instantly, a small hill appeared. Gun threw more Xirang at the hill, and the hill became a mountain. Water streamed off its sides as the mountain rose higher and higher. Gun was overjoyed! He began to throw the magic soil everywhere, and hills and banks formed, blocking the floodwaters.

As the water drained off the emerging land, people left the mountains to return to their homes. They saw Gun using Xirang to control the floods, and knelt on the ground in gratitude to him. Gun beckoned them to stand and join him. Soon, the plains and lowlands were completely transformed, and the water that was trapped between the hills and mountains started to evaporate.

Before long, news of what was happening on earth reached the Supreme God in heaven. He realised Gun had stolen the bowl of Xirang and leapt up from his throne in anger.

'How dare he disobey me!' he shouted. He ordered his soldiers to bring back the magic soil from the human world. Then he used his power to strike down Gun.

Gun was standing on Yu Mountain when he was struck down and killed by the power of heaven. After he fell to the ground, people laid his body on an altar and built a shrine in his memory. Because of their grief and sadness, they did not notice that the magical soil, Xirang, had disappeared from earth.

Without the power of Xirang, the floods again became uncontrollable, destroying houses and farmland. Yet the people had learned much from Gun and continued to fight against the floodwaters and the rains. They believed the spirit of Gun was still leading them, for his body still lay on the altar and had never perished. For three years, Gun's body remained unchanged, until news about it spread all the way to heaven.

When Tian Di found out that Gun's body had never decomposed, he began to worry that Gun would return to life and seek revenge. He ordered the God of Fire, Zhu Rong, to destroy the body once and for all.

Zhu Rong descended to earth in a giant ball of fire, scattering the people who had gathered at the shrine. He used his sword to cut into Gun's belly, but was startled to see a small dragon with sharp claws climb out of the opening. The dragon flew around the shrine, dodging Zhu Rong's attempts to catch him. Finally, it escaped out a window and disappeared into the sky.

Meanwhile, Gun's body had begun to twist around and change. Yellow scales covered his skin, and his shape transformed into the body of a dragon.

When Zhu Rong returned to the altar and saw the mighty yellow dragon, he fled back to heaven in fear.

The yellow dragon flew into a deep chasm near Yu Mountain and was never seen again.

The small dragon that climbed out of Gun's belly was actually his son. He later entered the human world and became the famous Yu. Yu taught the people how to dig channels and canals to divert the floodwaters into the sea. He completed the work that his father had begun.

Archer Yi and the Ten Suns

Long ago, when the earth was still new, there lived a god called Di Jun. Di Jun was the Supreme God of the East and he had two wives, Chang Xi and Xi He. Chang Xi, the mother of the moon, gave birth to twelve moons, while Xi He, the mother of the sun, gave birth to ten suns.

The ten suns lived with their mother in a place called Tanggu, far beyond the East Sea. Every morning before it was light, the ten suns would bathe in the waters of Tanggu, making it so hot that steam rose from the water's surface. At daybreak, one of the suns would ride in a chariot across the sky with his mother, Xi He. The chariot was pulled by six jade dragons, and as it crossed the sky the sun would shine on the earth below. At dusk, they returned to their home on the top of Fusang, a giant mulberry tree, and the sky would turn dark.

Back in these ancient times, a week was ten days long. On each day of the week, a different sun would ride across the sky in Xi He's chariot, while the others would rest in the branches of Fusang. The ten suns knew this was their duty, and they lived a happy and contented life with their mother.

Down on earth, people were grateful to the ten suns. They warmed the earth and brought vitality to all living things. To show their gratitude, people built shrines and offered prayers of thanks to the ten suns and their honourable parents.

However, after the passing of thousands of years, the suns became unhappy with their routine. They no longer wanted to wait for nine days until it was their turn to ride across the sky. So, one day, they decided to go into the sky together. They did not take their mother's chariot, but ran one after the other into the vast, expansive sky. Chasing after each other, the ten suns were so happy with their newfound freedom that they even forgot to return home.

Of course, this decision brought disaster to the earth. The power of the ten suns together scorched the land and shrivelled all the plants and crops. The treetops caught fire, and soon forests were ablaze all over the world. The searing heat evaporated rivers and lakes, leaving no water for the humans and animals to drink. In the course of a few days, the entire earth had become a dry wasteland, and life was in danger of becoming extinct.

At this time, the leader of the middle kingdom was Emperor Yao. When Emperor Yao saw the catastrophe created by the ten suns, he summoned all the people together and told them to pray to the Supreme God of the East, Di Jun. The people cried out to heaven and begged Di Jun to intervene.

Di Jun heard their cries and became greatly distressed. Never did he think his ten sons would act so selfishly and irresponsibly! He immediately ordered them to return to Fusang, but they refused. He asked his wife, Xi He, for assistance, but despite her pleas, the ten suns still refused to leave the sky.

'We no longer want to live according to the heavenly order,' they said. 'We want to live here, and be free to chase each other across the sky.'

Realising that he no longer had control over his sons, Di Jun called upon the help of Yi, a young god who lived in heaven. Di Jun hoped that Yi would be able to convince his sons to return. He gave Yi a red bow and a quiver of white arrows. 'I know that you are a great archer,' he said. 'My sons will not obey my orders to leave the sky, and they are destroying the earth. Use your power and bring them back to Tanggu.'

Yi immediately accepted his task. 'Do not worry,' he said. 'I will go down to earth and carry out your wish.'

Yi descended to earth, accompanied by his beautiful

wife, Chang E. But when Yi reached the human world and saw the destruction caused by the ten suns, he became very angry. Besides ruining the earth, they had also caused the deaths of many people. Everywhere he looked, Yi saw people dying and suffering from thirst and hunger.

Because Yi was a just god, he wanted the suns to pay for the damage they had done. He looked up at the sky, where the ten suns circled like great burning orbs. 'Go back home to Fusang immediately!' he said. 'By the order of your father Di Jun, you cannot stay here in the sky.' But the ten suns pretended not to hear Yi's order. Then Yi said, 'If you do not return, I will shoot you down.'

Yi shouted his threat to the ten suns several times, but they continued to ignore him and play in the sky. Furious, Yi grabbed his bow and arrow, took aim and shot at one of the suns. The wounded sun was like a giant fireball as it fell from the sky. When it reached the sea, it exploded in a cloud of steam, and a golden crow with three legs flew out from the vapours. The golden crow was the soul of the sun, and it quickly flew up to heaven.

After the first sun fell into the sea, the temperature dropped and all the people around Yi cheered.

Yi brought down eight more suns, one after the other, and eight more golden crows flew up to heaven. The remaining sun lessened its rays in fright, as if trying to hide from Yi. It dodged behind a great cloud and stayed there.

Yi realised that at least one sun was needed to give light and warmth to the earth. Lowering his bow and arrow, Yi turned to the people. 'If there is no sun in the sky, there will be no life in the world. You would not survive the darkness or cold. I think I should leave one in the sky.'

'You are right,' they replied. 'There must be one sun in the sky, so let this one stay!'

The last sun stayed in the sky and returned home at dusk to Tanggu. Ever since then, the sun never again dis-obeyed the heavenly order. It went to work every morning at dawn and returned to Tanggu at dusk, where it rested on Fusang at night. The earth recovered from the heat, and life began to thrive once again. Archer Yi became a hero for saving the earth, and all the people praised him.

The nine suns brought down by Yi's arrows fell into the East Sea. Their bodies formed a giant island of rock that stretched across an area of ten thousand kilometres. This island is called 'Wojiao'. The temperature on the island is so high that the air above it shimmers from the molten rock, and sea water instantly evaporates when it touches the shores, sending up clouds of steam.

How Chang E Flew to the Moon

Long, long ago, when the gods still walked the earth, there lived a young god by the name of Yi. Yi was a great archer, and he once saved the earth from endless heat by shooting down nine suns from the sky. The people on earth were so grateful to Yi, they gave him fragrant incense and sacrificial meats to present to the court of heaven.

Now, the father of the suns was Di Jun, the Supreme God of the East. When Yi returned to heaven, he went to Di Jun's throne and presented his gifts. But instead of being thankful, Di Jun became angry.

'You have killed nine of my sons!' he said. 'I ordered you to bring them back home, yet you destroyed all except for one. For this, you must take your wife to the human world and never return to heaven. I never want to see you again.'

Yi was greatly shocked. He had expected the Supreme God to thank him for saving the earth. It seemed unfair that he should be punished. But there was nothing he could do to change Di Jun's mind.

Yi left the court of heaven with a heavy heart. 'Didn't I save humans from destruction?' he asked his wife, Chang E, as they descended towards earth. 'If the nine suns had listened to me and returned home, I would not have shot them down. This punishment is unfair, for the suns were guilty, not I.'

But Chang E shook her head. 'You offended Di Jun because you killed his sons. Now I am being punished because of you. I can never return to heaven and be a goddess!' She began to weep. 'Don't you understand what this means? We will grow old and die if we live in the human world, for we can only be immortal when we live in heaven!'

Yi suddenly realised what he had done and was full of regret. On earth, he was welcomed as a hero, but it did not make him feel any better. Soon after they arrived, he decided to go hunting and took off into the forest alone on his horse.

When he returned after several days, Chang E greeted him at the door. 'I have great news,' she said. 'I have heard that a goddess called Xi Wang Mu lives on Kunlun Mountain. She has a potion that can make humans immortal. Perhaps she will give us some, and then we can return to heaven.'

Yi felt a surge of hope. 'If what you say is true,' he said, 'then I will go to Kunlun Mountain and beg Xi Wang Mu for the potion.'

'Be careful,' his wife warned. 'Kunlun Mountain is steep and full of danger. Many people have died trying to climb it.'

'No mountain can stop me,' Yi said confidently. 'I will leave tomorrow morning.'

The next morning at dawn, Yi shouldered his bow and arrows and readied his horse. He was determined to bring back the potion of immortality, no matter how difficult the task. He kissed Chang E goodbye and set off towards the west.

The sacred mountain of Kunlun stood at the end of a vast, rocky desert. Volcanoes surrounded it on all sides, spewing forth fire and molten lava that turned everything into cinder and ash. There was also a deep abyss at the foot of the mountain filled with water. Nothing could float on its surface, and boats that tried to cross it would immediately sink. The area was so dangerous that no mortal had ever managed to reach the mountain alive.

Yet Yi was no ordinary mortal. After journeying several days through the barren desert, he finally reached the beginning of the mountain range. Deep in the distance he saw the snow-covered peaks of Kunlun Mountain, encircled by volcanoes and red-hot lava.

Yi called upon his heavenly powers as he dismounted from his horse. Then he ran so quickly through the fiery landscape that the lava did not have time to burn him, nor did the showers of molten rock fall on him. When he reached the abyss of water at the foot of Kunlun Mountain, he jumped across it in a single bound and landed safely on the other side. Then he began his ascent to the peak of the mountain, to find the cave of Xi Wang Mu.

Xi Wang Mu was an ancient goddess, whose strange appearance would often change. Sometimes, she looked like a gentle old woman, while at other times she had a woman's body, but the tail of a leopard and the teeth of a tiger. She always wore a headdress known as 'sheng', which was made of gold and precious gems. Three huge bluebirds lived in her cave, and they gathered food for Xi Wang Mu, as well as the magical ingredients she used to make her potion of immortality.

When Yi arrived at her cave, Xi Wang Mu was greatly surprised. Here was an earthly man who had climbed Kunlun Mountain and survived! Yi told Xi Wang Mu why he had been exiled from heaven, and she nodded in understanding.

'Don't worry,' she said, 'for I don't think you should suffer for what you have done. Your contribution toward mankind is great, therefore I will give you a pill to restore your immortality.' Then she placed a round pill the size of a pearl in Yi's palm.

Yi was very grateful to Xi Wang Mu and thanked her many times. Now he and Chang E could become immortal again!

'This pill has taken me thousand of years to make, and there are special instructions for taking it,' Xi Wang Mu continued. 'You must divide it in half and take it with your wife on a special date. Only then will you both be able to fly back to heaven.' Xi Wang Mu bent close to Yi's ear and whispered the date to him.

Yi did not forget Xi Wang Mu's words as he journeyed down Kunlun Mountain. When he reached his home several days later, he showed the magic pill to his wife. She was filled with joy.

'But when can we take it?' she asked.

'Xi Wang Mu instructed us to wait for a certain date and then take it together,' Yi replied. 'Only in this way can we both return to heaven.' He gave Chang E the pill and told her to keep it safe until the special day arrived. However, he did not tell his wife when that date would be.

Since the day Yi left for Kunlun Mountain, Chang E had not stopped thinking about returning to heaven and resuming her life as a goddess. And now that the pill of immortality was in her possession, she became restless and impatient. As the days went by, she did not know how much longer she could wait. Finally, when Yi was hunting in the forest one afternoon, she took out the pill and swallowed it.

Immediately, she felt herself becoming lighter as she floated into the air. Escaping through an open window, she rose higher and higher into the sky.

Yi returned from hunting to see his wife fly out of the window. He ran to catch her. 'Chang E!' he shouted, reaching out his arms. 'What have you done?'

But Chang E could not answer him, for she was flying too quickly into the sky. As she rose above the earth, the sky grew darker and darker. She began to regret taking the pill alone and leaving Yi on earth. She knew that if she flew back to heaven without her husband, the other gods would accuse her of being selfish. She also knew she could not return to earth, for people would think she was cold-blooded and heartless. By then, Chang E had flown so high, she was approaching the moon. It shone brilliantly in the dark night, as if inviting Chang E to visit. So, with nowhere else to go, Chang E flew to the moon.

Just as she was about to land, she looked back at the earth. She saw her husband still holding his arms out towards her. He seemed to be trying to tell her something. But Chang E was too far away to hear him, and she landed on the white surface of the moon.

Chang E walked to the moon palace, but there was nobody there. At the back of the palace, she found a grove of cherry trees. There, under the trees, was a jade rabbit mixing medicine in a mortar and pestle. The rabbit

belonged to Xi Wang Mu, and he worked on the moon, preparing ingredients for the potion of immortality. Next to the rabbit was a toad, and these two animals were Chang E's only companions. Even today, if you look up at the full moon at night, you can still see the outline of a rabbit.

As for Yi, he was very disappointed that his wife had taken the magic pill by herself. He realised that he could neither return to the heaven nor be immortal. 'Then let me live with human beings forever and help them,' he said, and he lived the rest of his life on earth as an ordinary man.

How Meng Jiangnu Cried Down the Great Wall

During the years of China's first dynasty, the Qin Dynasty, there lived in a remote village two families by the names of Meng and Jiang. The two families were neighbours and they lived together in peace and harmony. However, neither the Meng family nor the Jiang family had any children, and this saddened them, for they did not want to grow old alone.

One day, Mr Meng planted a gourd seedling in his courtyard. The gourd vines grew quickly and spread over his lattice fence into the courtyard of his neighbour, Mr Jiang.

A few weeks later, Mr Jiang discovered a large gourd in his courtyard that had not been there the night before. Realising that the gourd was unusual, he went to find Mr Meng. 'You planted the vine,' said Mr Jiang, as he handed the gourd to his neighbour, 'so this belongs to you.'

Mr Meng thanked him and immediately carved up the gourd. To his surprise, there was a baby girl inside. She was as white as the colour of milk.

'Look at that, Jiang!' he shouted. He could hardly believe his good luck. Mr Jiang congratulated Mr Meng, for he finally had a daughter.

'But the vine grew in both our yards,' said Mr Meng. 'I shall call her Meng Jiangnu, so she has both our family names.'

By the age of eighteen, Meng Jiangnu was the most beautiful girl in the village. She was also very clever, for she read poetry and the ancient texts. Her fame soon spread throughout the region, and numerous matchmakers came to request her hand in marriage. But Meng Jiangnu refused them all.

One summer, when the weather was burning hot, Meng Jiangnu was having a bath in her courtyard. As she was bathing, she noticed that the leaves in the tree above her were shaking. Suddenly, she spotted a man in the tree, and she cried out in fear and grabbed her clothes.

'Who are you?' she shouted. 'I demand that you get down from that tree and show yourself!'

After a while, a young man climbed down from the tree. He was dressed as a scholar, and he approached Meng Jiangnu with his head bent towards the ground.

Meng Jiangnu was furious. 'What were you doing hiding in that tree? Who do you think you are?' she said.

But the scholar would not even look at her, and stood there blushing in shame. Finally, he stammered, 'Forgive me. My name is Fan Qiliang, and I was captured to work as a labourer on the Great Wall. I know that I would not survive the work camps, so I decided to run away. I have been using your courtyard to hide from the army. Please forgive me for offending you.'

Meng Jiangnu softened at once, for she had heard terrible stories about the labourers who were made to work on the Great Wall. She decided to ask her parents to help Fan Qiliang, and they readily agreed. From then on, Fan Qiliang lived at the Meng home.

Fan Qiliang was an honest and gentle man, and he worked hard at his studies. As each day passed, Meng Jiangnu admired the young scholar more and more.

One day, she decided to speak to him, for she knew that he was not yet married. 'I heard that only a husband can see a woman while she is bathing,' she said, blushing from her boldness. 'Did you see me bathing that day when you were hiding in the tree?'

Fan Qiliang immediately understood what Meng Jiangnu was asking. Taking her hand, he said, 'You are kind-hearted and beautiful, and I will be forever grateful for your help. But I am a fugitive, and if we marry you will be involved in my troubles.'

But Meng Jiangnu shook her head. 'I do not care. I want to marry you because you are honest and sincere. If you accept me as your wife, I will always follow you.'

Fan Qiliang was greatly moved by Meng Jiangnu's words and agreed to the marriage.

However, only a few days after their wedding, a young man who had hoped to marry Meng Jiangnu himself learned that Fan Qiliang was a fugitive. Filled with jealousy, he went and reported Fan Qiliang to the police.

That night, the wild barking of dogs woke up the newly wed couple. Before they could hide, a group of soldiers broke through the door and surrounded Fan Qiliang. As they put him in chains and dragged him away, Meng Jiangnu stood weeping by the door. 'I will find you again!' she cried, as she watched her husband disappear into the black night.

After his arrest, Fan Qiliang was forced to be a labourer on the Great Wall. Meng Jiangnu missed him dearly and waited for his return. But the weeks and years passed, and she never heard any news of her husband.

After many years, Meng Jiangnu's parents passed away, and she was left alone. Kneeling beside their tomb, she started to cry and vowed to find Fan Qiliang, no matter how difficult it might be. She asked for her parents' blessing to be reunited with her husband.

When she returned home, she wrapped up her belongings and the winter clothes she had made for Fan Qiliang, then set off on her journey on foot. She climbed over countless mountains and crossed dozens of rivers, yet still she pressed on. Through spring, summer and autumn, she continued on her journey until, one snowy winter day, she arrived at the foot of the Great Wall.

There, she saw many labourers in dreadful conditions, and the sight brought tears to her eyes. The labourers wore ragged clothes and had no shoes on their feet as they scaled the fortress with heavy baskets of stones. Meng Jiangnu asked every laborer she saw if they knew Fan Qiliang, but they all shook their heads, saying they had never heard of him. Then an old man approached her. 'Are you talking about the young fellow who could read and write?'

'Yes!' she shouted. 'Where is he?'

But the old man sighed and answered, 'He died almost a year ago. The army buried him under the Great Wall. I'm sorry.' Upon hearing this, Meng Jiangnu fainted and fell to the ground.

When she woke up, she was told that her husband had been treated very badly. Because he'd been a fugitive, he was made to do the heaviest work and was given only a small amount of food. After a few years, he became very sick, and was unable to work. Finally, he grew so weak that he died. He had been buried under the Great Wall, but no one knew the exact place.

Meng Jiangnu was determined to recover Fan Qiliang's body. But the Great Wall was five thousand kilometres long, so how would she ever find it? She was filled with such deep sorrow that she began to cry. Her sobs echoed through the mountains around the Great Wall. She cried for a long time. Then, with a great rumble, the Great Wall collapsed. Meng Jiangnu had brought down twenty kilometres of the Great Wall!

The debris and dust of the Great Wall exposed hundreds of white skeletons. For the first time they lay exposed in the air for all the labourers to see. Not knowing which skeleton belonged to her husband, Meng Jiangnu took out a sewing needle and pierced her finger. 'If you are my Fan Qiliang,' she called out to the trail of bones, 'then let my blood flow to your bones.'

As the drops of blood trickled from her finger, they flew in the wind towards one skeleton. Meng Jiangnu knew this skeleton belonged to her husband. She gathered the bones and gave her husband a proper burial.

News of the widow who had brought down part of the Great Wall soon reached the emperor. But when Meng Jiangnu was brought before him for judgement, the emperor decided not to punish her, for he was greatly impressed by her beauty.

'I have never seen a woman as beautiful as you,' he told her. 'I must have you as a concubine in my court.'

Meng Jiangnu refused and said, 'I demand to leave your palace.'

The emperor could barely conceal his anger. 'Although your loyalty to your husband is admirable,' he said, pretending to be concerned, 'it won't bring him back from the dead. If you agree to be my concubine, you will live in comfort for the rest of your life. Also, I will pardon you for your crime.'

Meng Jiangnu knew she would be executed by the emperor if she did not agree, so she told him, 'If you want me to be your concubine, then you must make three promises.'

'What promises are those?' he asked.

'First,' she replied, 'you must build a big tomb for Fan Qiliang; second, you and your ministers should attend his funeral; and third, you must hold a memorial ceremony for Fan Qiliang at the seaside.'

The emperor realised he had been tricked. If he said yes to Meng Jiangnu's conditions, then he would lose face. But if he refused, then she would be free to go. Finally, he agreed.

On the day of the Fan Qiliang's memorial ceremony,

Meng Jiangnu wore a white dress and walked at the head of the procession. The emperor and his ministers followed. When they reached the end of the Great Wall, where it stretched into the sea, Meng Jiangnu stopped and said, 'Qiliang, I have found you at last! The cruel emperor forces me to be his concubine, but I cannot go with him. I will join you in the underground world.' Then she turned around and pointed at the emperor. 'You are a terrible ruler,' she shouted. 'Although I can do nothing to harm your body, my death will eat away at your soul!' With this curse, Meng Jiangnu jumped off the Great Wall into the sea.

All of a sudden, the waves parted and two huge slabs of stone rose from the sea. One slab was tall, like a scholar's tablet, while the other was round. The round slab represented the watery tomb of Meng Jiangnu. After her death, the people of her village built a temple in memory of this heroic and virtuous woman.

Mulan

In the days when China was ruled by Southern and Northern Dynasties, there were many wars along China's northern border. This brought much distress to the people in the north, for whenever there was a war they had to flee their homes and villages to seek safety. Those who stayed suffered torture and death at the hands of the invaders. To protect its border from foreign attacks, Chinese officials decided to gather more soldiers at the frontline.

The Hua family lived in a small village near this northern border. Mr Hua was an old soldier who had fought in many battles when he was younger. Now, however, he had retired from the army and lived peacefully with his wife, his two daughters and his young son.

One day, the youngest daughter Mulan was inside working at her weaving machine when she heard the sound of horses' hooves approaching. After a series of rapid clops, the horses stopped outside her door. Mulan peeked out the window and watched as two officials dismounted and waited impatiently to be let inside. She quickly hid from view.

Mr Hua hurried to answer the loud knocks. He was nervous, as official visits never brought any good news.

'Welcome,' he said to the officials, trying to appear calm. 'How can we help you today?'

The tallest official stepped forward and answered, 'The enemy is again approaching our border. General He Yuting has ordered every man in the village to enlist in the army and serve in the frontline. This means that you,

Hua Hu, must leave your home immediately and join the army at the northern front.'

Mulan quickly stepped out from behind the door. 'Sir,' she said, nervously, 'my father is old and often sick. His health is not good enough for him to travel to the north, much less fight in the army. Please, at his age, don't you think he should be exempt?'

The official was furious. 'No!' he shouted. 'Do you dare ask your father to disobey the orders of the emperor?'

Mulan was about to reply when her father interrupted. 'Mulan,' he said, 'go inside, quickly!' He pulled the tall official outside and closed the door. 'Sir,' he said, 'I understand that the emperor is in need, and that each family must contribute –'

But the official wouldn't let him finish. 'If you cannot go, old man,' he said, 'then we will take your young son to replace you!' Horrified, Mr Hua watched as the officials stormed away to the next house, then he went back inside.

By evening, the news had disrupted the peace of the

entire household. Everyone was worried about the fate of their father. What were they to do? Mr Hua was clearly too old for fighting, and his health was not strong enough for him to travel to the harsh regions in the north. Yet how could they allow Mulan's younger brother, who was only seven years old, to go and fight in a battlefield?

As he sat smoking after the evening meal, Mr Hua was full of concern for the safety of his young son. Finally, he decided. He would leave the next morning and join the army. Rising slowly from his chair, he prepared himself to tell his family when Mulan suddenly jumped up from her weaving and ran towards him.

'Father,' she said, 'I have an idea! Each family has to contribute one man to the army, but younger brother is too young to go to the front, and you are too old. There-fore, let me dress as a man and use younger brother's name. No one would know!'

Mulan's father shook his head, anxiously. 'No,' he said. 'I cannot let you. It would be too dangerous.'

But Mulan would not give up. 'I have been learning

martial arts since I was young, and you know I'm good at fighting. Why not let me go?' Mulan's mother looked away, but her father was listening. 'Father,' she pleaded, 'you cannot go and younger brother is too small. What other choice do we have?'

After much persuading, Mulan's parents finally agreed, and the day of the big battle approached. Mulan prepared herself with weapons, clothes and armour. Sitting on top of the family's horse and dressed in her military outfit, Mulan looked like a handsome and elegant young soldier. No one would ever suspect that she was a girl. She said goodbye to her family and hurried on her way to join the army.

The army was marching northwards to launch an attack on the enemy. Riding to catch up with them, Mulan realised this was the first time she had been away from home. Tears sprang to her eyes, and her hands trembled as they held the reins. Mulan was worried the other soldiers would notice, but they were too focused on their goal of reaching the enemy camp.

After a day's travel, the army arrived at the banks of the Yellow River, the beginning of the northern frontier. The waves of the river rose and churned like ten thousand dancing lions, and Mulan imagined she could hear their roars as well. As she paced her horse back and forth along the river, she glanced south towards her home. She thought of her family, and silently made a vow to fight fearlessly for their protection.

Soon they heard the sound of horses, along with distant shouts and cries. The generals gave the order for the army to set up camp near the frontline. Everyone was tense at the thought of tomorrow's battle. Mulan, nervous and excited, could hardly sleep that night. She was filled with self-doubt, and woke up in a cold sweat. She was only a girl; what did she know about battle? What if she couldn't defend herself?

On their second day at camp, Mulan's army launched an attack on the enemy. The enemy soldiers responded with shouts of anger, and surged forward on their horses, their swords glinting in the sun. Mulan felt a stab of fear as they approached. In a matter of minutes, the soldiers were upon them. Suddenly, a swordsman on horseback charged towards her. Shielding herself from his blow, Mulan poised her spear and thrust it into his heart. The enemy fell off his horse, dead.

The first battle was soon over, and the battlefield was scattered with the bodies of enemy soldiers. That night, stories of Mulan's courage and skill in battle spread throughout the camp.

In the battles that followed, Mulan fought bravely, demonstrating her skill in both martial arts and weaponry. Because of her achievements, she was soon promoted, and hundreds of soldiers were placed under her command. The soldiers felt proud to fight alongside Mulan, as her courage as a warrior commanded deep respect.

Once, Mulan was accompanying General He in battle, when they fell victim to a surprise attack. In the middle of the battle, an enemy rider appeared next to General He and thrust a spear into his horse's leg. Injured, the horse buckled, and General He toppled to the ground. Turning

onto his back, General He saw an enemy soldier towering above him on horseback, ready to kill him. Just then Mulan appeared, and with a ferocious cry she killed the enemy with her spear. Then she quickly escorted General He out of danger.

Mulan went on to fight in hundreds of battles and win countless honours. After twelve years, the situation on the northern frontier had greatly improved. When the emperor heard the good news, he ordered that the warriors receive a reward and requested to personally meet the famous Mulan.

Upon arriving at court, Mulan was showered with treasures and gifts, greater than anything she had ever imagined. In addition, the emperor promised to appoint her as a minister in his court. Yet Mulan remained silent and only bowed her head in thanks. Then she quietly explained that she didn't want any fortune or title. She only wanted the emperor's permission to return home and visit her parents, whom she had not seen for more than twelve years.

The news of Mulan's triumphant return spread quickly

through her hometown. Her family prepared a huge feast, then dressed themselves in their best clothes. They waited anxiously at the city gate for her arrival.

When Mulan saw her family waiting for her, she almost leapt off her horse to embrace them. But she resisted the temptation, and instead slowly rode her horse to the old house she had left all those years ago. Once inside, she quickly greeted her family, then went to her old room. There, she took off her armour and her soldier's uniform, put on an old dress, and tied her hair back like a woman's.

When Mulan went outside again and faced the people in the village, everyone was shocked. No one would have believed that Mulan was just a girl, a girl who had won hundreds of battles as a soldier.

Many years later, a great poem was written about a young girl who chose to serve in the army for her father. Mulan had become a heroine for her bravery and skill in defending her country.

Mazu, the Goddess of the Sea

Over a thousand years ago, in a city on the coast of the Fujian province, there lived a military commander by the name of Lin Yuan. Lin Yuan's wife was pregnant, and on the twenty-third day of the third month of the Chinese calendar she went into labour. As the family gathered for the birth of the baby, a mysterious beam of red light appeared in the hallway and spread throughout the house, making everything glow with a soft, warm light. At the same time, a sweet fragrance, like the perfume of a thousand flowers, lingered in the air. Lin Yuan's family were greatly surprised, and they whispered excitedly about what these heavenly signs might mean.

It wasn't long before a midwife came out of the birthing room. 'Congratulations, Lord Lin!' she said. 'Your wife has just given birth to a healthy baby girl.'

Lin Yuan rushed into the room and saw his wife holding the new baby. But strangely, the baby wasn't crying. Instead, she had already opened her eyes and lay smiling at her mother and father.

For many days, the baby did not cry. In fact, for a whole month after the birth, Lin Yuan and his wife never heard their daughter make any sound at all! So they decided to name her 'Silent Girl', or Lin Moniang.

From the time she was very young, Lin Moniang displayed special talents. At the age of one, she would clasp her hands together and bow whenever she saw the statue of a god. At the age of five, she could recite long passages from the Buddhist scripts. And as soon as she went to school, her teachers exclaimed, 'Lin Moniang is so clever!

She understands everything.' She was also popular with her classmates because she was kind-hearted and always wanted to help others.

One day, Lin Moniang was playing at the seashore near her house. Suddenly, she heard a voice calling for help. Looking out at the sea, she saw a young boy struggling to keep his head above the waves. Lin Moniang knew he was close to drowning. She found an old, crumpled bamboo mat on the sand, picked it up and threw it in the water. Miraculously, as soon as she stepped on the mat, it became hard and stable like a wooden boat. Then she sailed towards the drowning boy and dragged him out of the water.

When Lin Moniang returned to the shore, a crowd of onlookers was waiting to help. They carried the boy ashore and praised Lin Moniang for her rescue. Soon, the news spread throughout the city, and people everywhere spoke of Lin Moniang's bravery and wisdom.

A year later, Lin Moniang's four brothers set off on a journey by boat. They worked as merchant traders and often travelled to faraway ports. On this particular journey, they encountered a ferocious storm that sent waves crashing against their boats. The storm was so big that even the people on shore were affected. The streets flooded and many houses by the seashore were swept away.

That night, as the rain and gusts of wind shook her house, Lin Moniang knelt before the Buddha's portrait. All of a sudden, she fainted and fell to the ground. Worried, her mother ran over and picked her up. Lin Moniang's body was ice cold and she seemed to have stopped breathing.

'Lin Moniang!' her mother shouted as she shook her body. 'Please don't die! Come back to me!'

At her mother's words, Lin Moniang uttered a small cry and balled up her hands in a fist. Water fell from her hands in small droplets, and then she stirred and sat up. 'Why am I not allowed to protect my brothers?' she asked, looking at the portrait of the Buddha. Then she hung her head and fell silent again. Her mother was greatly puzzled by her daughter's words.

Three days later, only three of Lin Moniang's brothers returned home; the eldest had drowned at sea. The surviving brothers explained that they had all sailed on different boats, yet all of their boats had met the huge storm. As their boats were about to capsize, a flying girl in red descended from the clouds and pulled the boats upright with her hands. However, the girl was not quick enough to save the last boat, the boat of the eldest brother, and it disappeared under the waves.

The family realised what had happened three nights before. Lin Moniang's spirit had left her body in the form of a flying girl to save her brothers from danger.

When Lin Moniang was twenty-eight, she had a dream that a merchant ship would run aground and all those onboard would drown. To save the shipmen, she climbed a mountain overlooking the sea in an attempt to guide the ship to shore. That night, a terrible thunderstorm raged across the land, and when people went to find Lin Moniang the next morning she had disappeared. Her body was never found.

Yet no one believed she had died in the storm, for there were those who claimed they had seen a girl in red fly up into the sky at the same time that the winds and rain had suddenly ceased. As the weather became calm, the clouds had turned as colourful as a rainbow and heavenly music had echoed across the sky. They believed that Lin Moniang, accompanied by fairies, had flown up to heaven and become immortal.

Since that time, there have been many stories of Lin Moniang helping those in danger at sea. Along the coastal regions of the South China Sea, people would report that they often saw a goddess in red flying over the waters. It was said that Lin Moniang watched over boats near the shore and guided them to safety in heavy fog with a red beacon. Not long after she disappeared from earth, Lin Moniang became known as Mazu, the Goddess of the Sea. Fisherman spoke of how the Goddess Mazu protected them by appearing at their masts whenever they called her name.

Even today, seafarers and fishermen still worship the

Goddess Mazu. If you visit the south-eastern coastal communities in China and Vietnam, you will find many temples and altars dedicated to her. All those who live by the sea consider her their benefactor and protector.

The Eight Immortals Cross the Sea

This is a story about seven men and one woman who achieved immortality though studying the ancient Taoist practices and martial arts. Chinese stories are filled with their adventures, and the 'eight immortals' are regarded as the protectors of the poor and unfortunate. They are also known for their strange behaviour and magical powers. Here is a famous myth about what happened when they decided to journey across the East China Sea.

One year, on the third day of the third lunar month, the Grand Empress invited the eight immortals to the Peach Banquet. The immortals had a wonderful time, feasting and drinking at the Grand Empress's table. When the banquet was over, they lay around, wondering what to do next. None of them wanted to return home, for they were eager for more adventures, so they decided to ride the clouds to the misty shores of the East China Sea.

When they arrived, Iron Cane Li, who always travelled with a magical iron cane, pointed towards the horizon. 'There lies the sacred island of Peng Lai. I have heard it is full of wondrous things. What do you say? Shall we go there?'

All the immortals agreed. Then Lu Dongbin spoke up. 'I have an idea,' he said. 'Instead of using clouds to cross the sea, why don't we use our respective powers? The practice would do us good.' The other immortals thought this was a good idea.

Iron Cane Li volunteered to go first. Although he was immortal, Iron Cane Li was a beggar who wore ragged, threadbare clothes and had a limp. Walking out towards the waves, he threw his iron cane into the sea and it became a boat with a ragged sail. He jumped into the boat and sailed rapidly forward, as if blown by a strong wind, though there was not the slightest breeze on land.

Zhang Guo Lao decided to go next. He was the eldest of the eight immortals, and he owned a magic donkey that neither ate nor drank. During the day, the donkey carried Zhang Guo Lao wherever he wanted to go. At night, Zhang Guo Lao patted the donkey on the back and it turned into a piece of paper. Zhang Guo Lao would fold up the paper and put it in his pocket before going to sleep. Now, stepping towards the sea, Zhang Guo Lao took out his paper donkey. He puffed out his cheeks and blew on the paper, and it turned into a real donkey. Jumping onto it, he turned around so that he could wave to his companions as he rode out to sea facing backwards. They laughed and waved back.

There were six immortals left. Zhongli Quan started to get worried. He was the fattest of the immortals and never wore a shirt, preferring to show off his huge, shining belly. He was also very lazy. His magic object was a palm-leaf fan. Placing his fan on the water, he watched as it grew until it was ten feet across. Then he lay down on the fan and floated across the sea.

Next, it was Han Xiang Zi's turn. He carried a small magical flower basket, which he'd once used to teach a greedy emperor a lesson. Using his bottomless basket, Han Xiang Zi had emptied the state treasury and given the money to the poor. Now, he approached the sea and floated his basket on the water. The other immortals watched in amusement as Han Xiang Zi gingerly put one foot in the basket, then the other. Standing upright, Han Xiang Zi sailed over the waters.

Now there were only four immortals left. Lu Dongbin stepped forward with his sword. Holding it above his head, he called on his thunder magic to help him. The sword began to glow with a blinding light, and Lu Dongbin pointed it towards the island. Suddenly, he was lifted into the air by the power of the sword and he flew away.

Royal Uncle Cao volunteered to go next. He was the

fiercest of the immortals and the others trembled at his temper. He took out his jade tablet and, in a booming voice that shook the ground, he began to read a spell. The tablet started hovering over the water. Uncle Cao quickly grabbed hold of the tablet and it carried him over the sea.

Next was He Xiangu, a beautiful woman who ate a magic peach and became an immortal fairy. Fairy He always carried a giant lotus flower, and the flower had the ability to calm violent storms and shelter people from harm. Fairy He walked gracefully to the edge of the water and floated her lotus flower. Then she stood in the middle of the flower and waved to Lan Caihe as she floated away.

Lan Caihe was the only immortal left on land. He had an array of magical instruments, but his favourite was a pair of jade castanets. No one could resist the enchanting rhythms when Lan Caihe played his castanets. Even arrows in mid-flight had been known to stop and change their direction. Now, Lan Caihe struck up such a powerful rhythm that the air lifted him from the ground and took him across the sea.

When the immortals reached the island, they realised Lan Caihe was missing. They waited for him to appear, but soon began to worry. 'Something is wrong,' said Iron Cane Li. 'And I bet the Dragon King knows what has happened. Let's pay him a visit.'

The others agreed and flew back to the depths of the East Sea, where they demanded to talk to the Dragon King. Before long, a small dragon surfaced from the dark waters, surrounded by an army of crabs and shrimp.

'I am the third son of the Dragon King,' he said crossly. 'Why are you making so much noise?'

'We are looking for the immortal Lan Caihe,' said Iron Cane Li. 'Do you know where he is?'

The dragon cast his big eyes over the immortals, then said, 'I was sleeping under the sea when the sound of his jade castanets disturbed me. So I've locked him up in the Dragon Palace. There is nothing you can do.'

Lu Dongbin was outraged. 'We demand the release of Lan Caihe now!' he shouted, wielding his sword above his head.

The dragon and Lu Dongbin began to fight, but the dragon was no match for the immortal's skill. Soon, he was badly injured and had no choice but to promise the release of Lan Caihe. Wounded, he retreated back to his underwater palace.

Lan Caihe was set free and joined the other immortals on the island, but he was still upset. 'The dragon refused to give me back my jade castanets!' he said.

All the immortals wondered what they should do. Finally, Iron Cane Li had an idea. He took out his magic flask, uncapped the top, and a stream of fire gushed out. Han Zhongli began to fan the flames with his palm leaf, and soon the entire East Sea was on fire. The waters started to boil, and the Dragon King and his family fled from their palace.

The eight immortals descended into the empty palace and found Lan Caihe's jade castanets in the treasure room. But when they returned to the surface, the Dragon King was waiting for them with an army of warriors.

A ferocious battle began that lasted for many hours.

The immortals were powerful, but they were outnumbered by the Dragon King's warriors. It seemed like neither side could win.

All of a sudden, a voice from the sky shouted, 'Stop!' Everyone looked up and saw it was the Goddess of Mercy. As she descended from the heavens, she poured nectar over the burning sea, extinguishing the flames. Both the Dragon King and the immortals were immediately subdued, for no one dared to argue with the goddess.

The Dragon King apologised for his son's behaviour and asked forgiveness from the immortals. They regretted burning the Dragon Palace and promised to help the Dragon King rebuild. Satisfied that peace had been restored, the goddess ascended back to heaven.

Tired from their efforts, the eight immortals went to rest on the island. The next morning, they decided to return to the human world. They also decided not to drink so much peach wine the next time they attended the Grand Empress's Peach Banquet!

Why Kua Fu Chased After the Sun

A long time ago, when gods and goddesses still visited the earth from heaven, there lived a tribe of giants. The giants' home was a majestic mountain high above the great plains of northern China. No one had ever climbed the mountain, but everyone knew that giants lived there, because their booming voices thundered across the plains and their heavy footsteps shook the houses at the mountain's base. But the people were not afraid of the giants, for they were kind-hearted and gracious. They also had a reputation for being stubborn. When a giant decided to do something, it was often impossible to change his mind.

One of the giants was called Kua Fu, and he wanted to accomplish a great deed. Kua Fu normally spent his days fishing and hunting and his nights sleeping under the stars, but one day he had a rather extraordinary idea. He was walking through the grasslands of the north when he looked at the sky and saw the sun heading west towards the horizon. He knew that dusk would soon arrive, as the red sun no longer burned but instead cast a calm, gentle light over the ground. Yet Kua Fu could not take pleasure in the sunset. Instead, he became nervous, for he did not like night.

'The sun is setting and soon it will be dark. The long night is so unbearable that I can't stand it!' Kua Fu said to himself. 'How I wish it would stay daylight forever.'

As he watched the setting sun, he began to wonder where the sun was going. Then he had an idea. 'Perhaps I can keep it in the sky?'

Excited by this thought, Kua Fu decided to run after the sun to find out where it went after it had set. 'If I catch up with the sun,' he reasoned, 'then I'll be able to know the truth about night and day. And perhaps I can convince the sun to stay in the sky during the night!'

So, Kua Fu stretched his long legs and began to run after the setting sun. His strides became bigger and bigger, and he ran faster and faster. Soon, he was sweeping across the plains like the wind, and sometimes he even flew over the land, so great was his speed. Eventually, he started to catch up with the sun.

The house of the setting sun was called Yu Gu. It was a great abyss with no end. Once the sun was inside Yu Gu, all of its rays of light were swallowed by the darkness, causing night to fall.

Now, the sun had just passed over the edge of Yu Gu and was about to plunge into the darkness. As he ran towards it, Kua Fu held out his arms and shouted the sun's name. The sun was surprised to hear a voice calling and slowed its descent, hovering above the darkness of Yu Gu.

Kua Fu had almost reached the edge of Yu Gu when he stopped to take a good look at the sun. It was larger than anything he had ever seen, and it glowed red and bright like a gigantic fireball. As he thought about the light and vitality the sun gave to the world, he suddenly exclaimed, 'What a truly amazing thing the sun is!'

Kua Fu continued his walk towards the sun until his body was covered over with sunshine. He began to glow a golden, red colour, just like the sun. Kneeling at the edge of Yu Gu, he said, 'Sun, I've done it! I've caught up with you. Don't go down into Yu Gu. Just let me hold you in my arms so that you'll stay here in the sky.'

Kua Fu raised his arms to embrace the sun, when all of a sudden he felt a searing pain through his body. He became thirsty, thirstier than he had ever felt in his life. Although his hands were just about to touch the sun, Kua Fu had to stop, because all he could think about was water.

Searching around him, Kua Fu saw the Yellow River in the distance. He turned away from the sun and ran towards the river, desperate to have a drink. With only a few gulps, Kua Fu emptied the entire river. But the pain of thirst still burned in his body, so he ran towards the mighty Wei River. Soon, Kua Fu had drained the mighty Wei River as well. Yet he was still thirsty.

Then Kua Fu remembered Big Lake in the north, which was right next to his mountain home. Big Lake was also called the 'endless sea', for it had an infinite amount of sweet lake water. Kua Fu knew that he had to reach Big Lake, for only there would he find enough water to stop his burning thirst.

He began to run back towards the north, but soon felt tired. Exhausted by his chase with the sun and scorched by its golden rays, he had to slow his pace. Looking down, he saw a golden peach tree, so he uprooted the tree and used it as a walking stick. Now his strides were becoming shorter and shorter and his pace slower and slower. With every step he took, Kua Fu's thirst grew stronger, until finally he could only take one small step at a time.

At last, Kua Fu saw Big Lake ahead in the distance,

but he could no longer take even one more step forward. With an enormous crash that echoed throughout the lands, Kua Fu collapsed to the ground like a falling mountain. From where he lay, he looked up at the setting sun. The afterglow of the sun's rays fell on his face and soothed him. He heaved a deep sigh, and with his last bit of strength threw his walking stick towards the river. Then, knowing that he had caught up with the sun and succeeded, Kua Fu closed his eyes and breathed his last breath.

The body of Kua Fu became a high mountain. The walking stick he threw towards the river became a forest of peach trees. Every summer after Kua Fu died, the trees produced many fresh peaches, and the peaches gave strength and perseverance to those who ate them. These gifts were given by the gods to human beings, so that they could remember Kua Fu and have the strength to carry out their dreams.

Gao Liang and the Dragon King

Long, long ago in ancient times, all the water in the world was controlled by dragons. Dragon Kings ruled over the seas, lakes and rivers, and they also controlled the movement of floods and tides.

One such dragon lived in Beijing. At this time, Beijing was not the capital of China, but it was already a bustling city filled with people from all over Central Asia. The city was so large that people could enter it through ten different gates. To help manage all the people, city officials divided Beijing into an inner city and an outer city.

One day, the emperor decided to make the inner city the capital of China. But the inner city was still connected to the sea, so there were many parts that were full of water. The emperor went to find the Dragon King.

'I want to build my capital here,' he said. 'So you must move this water beyond the walls of the inner city. I am the emperor, so you must do what I say!'

The Dragon King was not happy with this order, but he dared not defy the emperor. With a swish of his enormous tail, he dived into the water. Then he swam with great speed to the outer city, bringing all the water with him.

The emperor ordered the construction of new buildings, and soon the inner city was grand enough to be the capital of China. But the emperor was not satisfied. He wanted to continue building in the outer city to make his capital bigger. He summoned the Dragon King again.

'I want to extend my capital into the outer city,' he said. 'You must remove the water immediately.'

But the Dragon King shook his head angrily. 'My palace is in the outer city,' he said. 'It is impossible for me to move the water.'

At this, the emperor became furious. 'What?' he shouted. 'Do you dare defy my orders? If you don't move your palace within three days, then we will build over it and trap you underneath!'

Three days later, the Dragon King still had not moved from his palace in the water. So the emperor ordered that the new city wall be built directly on top. The throne room of the Dragon King and Queen was now buried under the city gates. This made entering and exiting the Dragon Palace very inconvenient.

Finally, the Dragon Queen could not stand it any longer. 'We have to move!' she said to her husband. 'It's impossible to live this way.'

Reluctantly, the Dragon King agreed, but then he thought of a way to get his revenge. 'When we move, we'll take all the water in the city with us,' he said. 'Not a single drop will be left, and the emperor and the entire city of Beijing will die of thirst!'

With that, the Dragon King went and found two magic wooden barrels. Although the barrels were not very big, they could hold an infinite amount of water. Together, the Dragon King and Queen gathered all the water in Beijing into the barrels and set them on a wheelbarrow. Then the Dragon King changed himself into an old man, and the Dragon Queen became an old woman. Before dawn, they left Beijing through the western city gate, pushing the wheelbarrow in front of them. Their load was heavy because of the water and they moved very slowly.

Not long after dawn, the city builders began their work and discovered that all the water in the city was gone. When the emperor heard the news, he realised the Dragon King had stolen it. He ordered his soldiers to immediately close the city gates and be on the lookout for anyone suspicious. Then he summoned the city counsellor. 'You are responsible for getting the water back,' he said.

The soldiers searched everywhere, but could not find the water. Soon they heard reports that an old man and woman had been seen taking a wheelbarrow with two barrels of water through the western gate. 'That must have been the Dragon King and the Dragon Queen,' said the counsellor. 'We have to stop them.'

The counsellor summoned Gao Liang, a young and fearless general, and told him what had happened. 'Gao Liang,' said the counsellor, 'you are skilled at martial arts so I will assign this task to you. You must catch up with the Dragon King and Queen and bring the water back to the city. If you fail, Beijing will become a dry, waterless city and all the people will perish from thirst.'

'But how can I bring the water back?' Gao Liang asked, anxiously. 'The Dragon King and Queen are very powerful. It is too difficult a task for me alone.'

'When you catch up with the king and queen, try to convince them to return the water on their own,' said the counsellor. 'But if they refuse, then use your spear and pierce through one of the barrels and all the water will flow back to Beijing. Remember, the barrel on the right contains sweet water and the one on the left contains bitter water, so only pierce the barrel on the right. The water will gush out in an enormous river, so you must ride ahead of it. And make sure you never look back.'

Gao Liang considered the counsellor's words. 'I understand,' he said. 'As soon as I pierce the barrel, the river of water will run towards the city. I must ride ahead of it, otherwise it will overtake me.'

'That's right,' said the counsellor. 'We will keep the western gate open until you return. As long as you ride straight towards the gate, you will be fine. Now go quickly!'

'Don't worry,' said Gao Liang. 'I will return with the water.' Then he took up his spear and galloped out through the western gate.

Before long, he saw a tall willow tree with two pairs of footprints underneath it. 'The Dragon King and Queen must have rested here,' he thought. 'Maybe they are not too far away.' And he spurred his horse onwards.

After a while, he spotted an old man and an old woman pushing a wheelbarrow. The old man was sweating and the old woman could hardly catch her breath. Gao Liang knew they were the Dragon King and Queen, and he galloped towards them, shouting, 'Stop! Stop!'

The Dragon King heard Gao Liang's approach and pushed the wheelbarrow forward even harder. Yet he was no match for Gao Liang's horse and soon Gao Liang stood in front of them, blocking their way.

'Dragon King,' he shouted, 'you cannot take the water away from Beijing. I order you to return it at once! If you do, then the emperor will not punish you or the Dragon Queen.'

But the Dragon King would not be convinced. 'Look here!' he said, angrily. 'I am the Dragon King. I'm the one who's in charge of the water, not the emperor!'

'Yes,' said the Dragon Queen, 'the water is ours. This affair has nothing to do with you, so leave us alone.'

This made Gao Liang's temper flare. 'If you don't do what I say,' he threatened, 'then I will use force.' He charged at the Dragon King and Queen with his spear, but they ran behind the barrels for protection. Then Gao

Liang remembered what the counsellor had said and thrust his spear into one of the barrels.

But he made a mistake! In his haste, he speared the barrel on the left with the bitter water. With a loud gushing sound, the water flowed out of the barrel. Gao Liang quickly turned his horse and galloped back towards the western gate. Behind him, the mighty river followed close on his heels, roaring like thunder.

By the time Gao Liang neared the western gate, it was already dark. He saw the torches alight on the gate tower and thought happily, 'I've made it! I have brought the water back!' Without thinking, he looked behind him. The water immediately rushed over his head and swallowed him completely.

When they saw what had happened from the top of the tower, the counsellor and his soldiers cried out. They rushed down to help Gao Liang, but they were too late. He had already drowned. The people were filled with sadness. They knew Gao Liang was a hero who had sacrificed his life to save those in Beijing from thirst. In order to remember him, they named the new river created by the rushing water Gao Liang He, or 'Gao Liang River'. Then they built a small bridge over the river and called it Gao Liang Qiao, or 'Gao Liang Bridge'. Even today, if you go to Beijing, you will see a small bridge named Gao Liang Qiao that stands just outside the western gate at the place where Gao Liang died.

As for the Dragon King and Queen, they continued their journey westward with the remaining barrel of sweet water, until they reached Jade Spring Mountain. As they were too exhausted to push the water any longer, they decided to pour it out at the foot of the mountain. Since that time, people come to Jade Spring Mountain to collect sweet water, for the water in Beijing is too bitter to drink.

The Epic of Jianger Khan
A MONGOLIAN MYTH

During the time of the ancients, when the gods still walked among men, a hero was born in the human world. His name was Jianger Khan, and he was the ruler of the Mongolian kingdom of Baomuba.

There are many famous legends about Jianger Khan. Some say that when he was only three, he defeated the ferocious leader of the Manggusi tribe in battle, and at the age of four, he cut four passageways through the northern mountains with his axe. Then, at the age of five, he captured the five demons that terrorised the Tahei Kingdom, and at the age of six he became the commander-in-chief of Baomuba's army. By the time he was seven, they say he had conquered the seven enemy nations that surrounded his kingdom. With the help of his powerful army, Jianger went on to establish a nation with forty-two kingdoms in its command.

Under Jianger's rule, Baomuba became rich and prosperous, and its people rejoiced in the beauty of their kingdom. Across the lands of Mongolia, it was known as a paradise on earth, for the people of Baomuba lived for hundreds of years and yet never looked older than twenty-five. Their homes were made from the wood of evergreen trees that never needed repairing. And no matter how cold the wind was outside, the houses were always as warm as spring sunshine.

One day, Jianger Khan's six thousand soldiers decided to construct a palace. 'We will make a home for our ruler that is beyond compare,' they said, and set off to find the most skillful architects in the kingdom. They ordered the architects to build a ten-storey golden palace in the middle of Baomuba. When it was finished, it stood only three fingers lower than the sky. The outside walls were decorated with gems and crystals, while mirrors covered the inside walls, reflecting the flames of thousands of lamps. The floor was made of polished red coral. The palace was so splendid that it shone as bright as the sun; there was no other palace on earth like it. Soon, news of the spectacular palace had spread and the kingdom was even more admired.

But there was one king who was filled with jealousy every time he heard about the palace of Baomuba. This king's name was Huluku, and he plotted for a way to invade the rival kingdom. One day, he learnt that Jianger and his warriors had left on a faraway mission, so he gathered a huge army of men and set off to attack Baomuba.

Jianger's brother, Honguer, had been left in charge of the palace. He was standing on the turret at dusk when he saw the lights from thousands of torches. It was Huluku's army. Honguer was a skilled archer and he immediately shot an arrow into the sky. With only three arrows, he managed to pierce through the heads of fifty soldiers.

As the arrows continued to rain down, Huluku became frightened. He sent three archers into the palace to kill Honguer by surprise. As Honguer defended the palace, the archers shot at him from behind. One arrow lodged in Honguer's right arm, and as he tried to pull it out the rest of Huluku's army stormed the palace doors. Soon Honguer was surrounded by six thousand swords and seventy spears, and he had no choice but to surrender. King Huluku bound Honguer with thick ropes and imprisoned him in the seventh hell at the bottom of the Red Sea. Eight thousand guards were placed in front of his cell, and every day they gave Honguer eight thousand lashes from their whips and eight thousand cuts from their knives.

After Honguer was taken prisoner, Huluku took control of Baomuba and his army ransacked the once beautiful kingdom.

When Jianger heard what had happened to his beloved brother, he was filled with rage. He made an oath to the gods that he would rescue Honguer and reclaim his kingdom. Then he swore revenge against the evil king Huluku.

After travelling to the furthest edge of the horizon, Jianger finally reached the seventh hell. At the entrance, he was approached by a mysterious woman. 'What is your name?' she asked. But Jianger knew she was a female demon and would eat him if he spoke, so without saying a word he swung his sword and cut off her head. Then he came upon a dark hut. When he entered inside, seven small ghosts pounced on him from all directions. Again Jianger swung his sword, but the seven ghosts were too quick and he couldn't strike a single one. So he took out his rope and caught them all in a single lasso. Then he tied them up and blew in their faces, for ghosts cannot stand the breath of humans. Instantly, their heads turned to ashes.

After defeating the seven small ghosts, Jianger went to leave the hut when he heard a voice. 'You killed my mother and seven brothers, so I will not let you leave here,' it said. Jianger searched the hut for the owner of the voice, but he couldn't see anyone. Where had the

sound come from? All of a sudden, an even smaller ghost jumped out of a cradle. The ghost was the size of a three-month-old baby.

Although the ghost had just been born, it was not easy to kill. Despite his best efforts, Jianger could not harm the baby ghost. It dodged his sword and ran out of the hut, making Jianger chase it throughout the lands of the seventh hell. For twenty-four days they fought, until finally Jianger saw that the ghost wore a small mirror on a chain near his heart. 'That must be his weakness,' thought Jianger, and he drew his knife and threw it at the mirror. The tip of the knife shattered the mirror and pierced the chest of the ghost. The baby ghost was dead.

As Jianger picked up his knife, he heard the sound of Buddhist scriptures being chanted. He followed the sound over many mountains until he arrived at a tall tree with leaves that shone like green stars. Jianger knew the tree was sacred, so he climbed its branches and carefully picked twenty of the shining leaves. Then he stored them in his bag.

At the end of all these challenges, Jianger finally reached the bottom of the Red Sea, where his brother was imprisoned. The eight thousand guards rushed towards him, and Jianger fought against them bravely for six days and six nights. At the end of the sixth night, he used his sword to kill the last guard.

Now that all the demons, ghosts and guards were dead, Jainger went to find his brother. But when he arrived at Honguer's cell, he saw only a pile of green grass. At that moment, he knew that Honguer's body had perished from the torture of the guards and become grass. With a cry of sadness, Jianger gathered up the green grass in his bag. Then he cut a hole in the top of the cell and swum upwards through the waters of the roaring Red Sea. He used all his strength to force his way through the water, for the heaviness of the sea pulled at his body and crushed his lungs. All the while, he held tightly to his bag with the green grass.

Once he was back on land, Jianger planted the grass in the earth. Then he took out the leaves from the sacred tree, chewed them in his mouth and spat them on the grass. Miraculously, Honguer's skeleton appeared. Jianger chewed more leaves and put them over the bones, and soon the bones were covered with flesh. Finally, Jianger placed two sacred leaves over Honguer's eyelids and they gradually opened.

Jianger was overjoyed that his brother was alive again. He helped Honguer stand up and hugged him tightly. Then the two brothers rode back to Baomuba together. When King Huluku saw them approaching in the distance, he sent his army out to kill them. But the army was no match for Jianger's sword and Honguer's arrows, and soon the evil king was defeated. The two brothers reclaimed the palace, and once again the Kingdom of Baomuba became a place of peace and beauty.

Meanwhile, the tale of Jianger has been passed down by the Mongolian people from generation to generation. Even today, it remains one of the most important stories about their history.

Camel Spring

A Sala Myth

Over seven hundred years ago, during the reign of the Yuan Dynasty, there was a small city by the name of Samarhan. In this city lived two brave and honest brothers called Ahemang and Galemang. The brothers were good businessmen and skilled at trading, so they soon became the leaders of their tribe. Under their leadership, the tribesmen lived happier and more prosperous lives.

However, not everyone in Samarhan was happy with the growing status of the two brothers. The noblemen and their families were especially annoyed, for they envied the achievements of Ahemang and Galemang. They also disliked the way the brothers gave money to the poor, for they wanted to keep all the wealth to themselves.

One day, they took their complaint to the king of Samarhan. 'Your majesty,' they said, 'the two brothers Ahemang and Galemang are really devils in disguise. They are only here to cause unrest among the people. If they succeed, they will take over your throne.' The king listened to the noblemen in dismay and then asked for their advice. 'The only way for the country to remain at peace is if the brothers are dead,' they warned.

The king and his ministers discussed how to be rid of the two brothers. It was decided that Ahemang and Galemang would be arrested and executed the following day.

That night, Ahemang dreamt that a wise old scholar was speaking to him. 'Those in high positions are often attacked,' the scholar said. 'You should not stay here, but instead gather your people and travel to the east. Be sure to take a white camel with you.' Ahemang awoke from his dream in a cold sweat. Frightened, he woke up his brother.

'But I've had the same dream too!' Galemang said. The two brothers decided to leave the city immediately.

In the dark of the night, they woke up the other members of their tribe and told them to prepare for a journey. Then they selected the one white camel from their herd. They also took a pot of clear spring water and a bag of fertile soil from the ground. After strapping their holy book to the white camel, they bowed three times to the east, and set off on their journey.

When the king's men arrived at the tents to arrest Ahemang and Galemang, they were surprised to find there was no one there, not even the tribesmen and their families. They hurried back to tell the king. After many months had passed and there was still no news of the brothers and their tribe, the king slowly forgot all about them.

Meanwhile, the journey to the east was long and difficult for the two brothers and their people. After they had climbed twenty-nine steep mountains and crossed

twenty-nine treacherous rivers, they finally reached Wu Tusi Mountain on the bank of the Yellow River. As Ahemang looked at the rocky face of the mountain and the raging waters of the river, he sighed. 'This will be our thirtieth mountain and thirtieth river,' he said wearily to Galemang.

'Then let us camp here,' Galemang decided. 'We will restart our journey tomorrow, after everyone has rested.'

As the daylight faded, the tribesmen busied themselves preparing the camp. Just before dark, they discovered the white camel that carried the holy book was missing.

'The white camel is gone!' they shouted, as they ran towards Ahemang and Galemang.

The two brothers took up burning torches and ordered the others to join them in a search for the camel. All through the night they searched on the slopes of Wu Tusi, and found nothing. Finally, at daybreak, one of the men spotted something white amongst the reeds that grew alongside the Yellow River.

Thinking they had found the camel, the group ran

towards the spot. But as they got closer, they saw that it wasn't the white camel at all, but a snow-white rock. However, strapped to the side of the rock was their holy book.

Ahemang and Galemang looked closer and saw that a spring of clear, sweet water flowed from a crack in the rock. Tears of gratitude came to their eyes. 'Didn't the old scholar tell us to bring the white camel?' Galemang said. 'Was it not a hint that the white camel would lead us to our destination?'

The two brothers climbed up a hill to look at the landscape below. Dense forest covered the mountains, appearing purple in the misty morning air. On both sides of the Yellow River, there were plains and wide fields.

Galemang took out the pot of spring water from their homeland and saw that the water from the white rock was just as clear and sweet. Then he knelt down and scooped up a bit of earth from the riverbank. When he compared it to the soil from their homeland, he discovered that it was the same in colour and fertility. This was indeed the land they had been looking for. They had found their new home! The two brothers held the holy book high above their heads, and all the tribesmen cheered.

Soon Ahemang and Galemang discovered that their new home had not only sweet water and fertile land, but also honest and kind-hearted people. The Tibetans who lived on the mountain welcomed the brothers and their tribesmen. The nearby Mongolians were also generous, and offered the tribe some of their land and sheep. The two brothers and their tribe spread across the lands and lived there for generations.

Even today, a white stone in the shape of a camel lies among the reeds and flowers of the spring, which the tribespeople named 'Camel Spring', in memory of the white camel that led them to their new home. Every year, the descendants of those tribespeople go on a pilgrimage to Camel Spring to pay respect to their ancestors who immigrated there from afar, and to remember the magical story of their heritage.

The Kung Fu Master

In Beijing, during the late years of the Qing Dynasty, there lived a kung fu master called Dong Haichuan. He invented a new kind of kung fu called 'Eight Diagram Boxing', which was different to other types of kung fu. Whenever he practised his kung fu, Dong would walk around in a circle, getting faster and faster, yet he never missed a step. As he walked, he raised and lowered his arms to create sixty-four different poses.

Dong's style of kung fu became famous, and he soon

had many disciples and students. The new style helped people to become physically strong and learn martial arts skills. It also taught them how to fight. 'But people learning kung fu should abide by kung fu ethics,' Dong would tell his students. 'You should never use it to harm or bully others.' He advised them to use their skills only for defence.

One day, Dong was teaching his disciples at the Heavenly Temple in Beijing. As they practised their kung fu in the park beside the temple, people gathered around to look at the unusual style. Suddenly, a tall man in the crowd burst into loud laughter. 'Ha!' he shouted. 'Walking around and around like that is not kung fu. You look like a blind man trying to find something in the dark!'

On hearing the man's insults, the disciples became angry. 'You don't know what you are talking about,' they said. 'Leave us alone and let us practise!'

But the man would not go away and continued to taunt them. 'I'm laughing because you don't know real kung fu,' he said.

162

At that, one of the disciples walked up to him. 'How dare you laugh at us!' he shouted, and they began to fight.

Dong saw the fight and ran towards them. 'Stop!' he yelled, and stepped between them. 'Why are you fighting here?'

'This man insulted our practice!' answered his disciple. 'I'm trying to teach him a lesson.'

Dong ordered his disciple to step back and approached the man. 'Who are you?' he asked.

The stranger looked at Dong and said smugly, 'I am Zhang Hu, and I also practice kung fu, but not this silly form you are doing. I will show you my kung fu.'

With that, Zhang walked towards a tall stone monument in the park. He stripped off his clothes, showing his powerful muscles to the crowd. 'Look at my strength!' he shouted, and grabbed hold of the monument. With little effort, he pulled the monument out of the ground and threw it aside. The audience all clapped their hands and shouted, 'Bravo! Bravo!'

Yet Dong remained calm. 'You have great strength,'

he said to Zhang. 'I tell you what, if you can move me, then you will be my master.'

Zhang readily agreed and stepped back. Meanwhile, Dong planted his legs firmly on the ground and stood with his arms bent. Zhang ran towards him at full force, trying to push him to the ground. But when he hit Dong, the kung fu master didn't move. The crowd laughed, for it looked like Zhang had just tried to push a wall.

'Why, you!' shouted Zhang as he backed away. Again and again, he ran towards Dong, and each time, he failed. He became angrier and angrier. Finally, Zhang decided to surprise Dong by attacking his legs. This time, Dong straightened his arms and pushed Zhang away. Zhang immediately fell backwards, tumbling to the ground. The audience burst into impressed applause.

Dong walked over and helped Zhang stand up. 'Sorry,' Dong said, and offered Zhang his hand. But Zhang was furious. Red-faced, he snatched up his shirt and stormed away without saying a word.

Meanwhile, the disciples surrounded their master,

praising him for his defence. 'That Zhang is so arrogant,' they said. 'He should be taught a lesson!'

But Dong shook his head. 'That is not the way of kung fu,' he said, and ordered his disciples to resume their practice.

Now, even though Zhang had lost the contest with Dong, he would not give up, for he was very stubborn. That night, he went to the house of a thief and bought a pistol. Then he went to find Dong's house. From outside the house, he peered through a window and saw Dong sitting on the floor in meditation. He took out his pistol, aimed at Dong and squeezed the trigger. The gunshot reverberated through the neighborhood and sent up a cloud of smoke in front of Zhang's eyes. Yet when the smoke cleared from the room, Dong was not there!

Suddenly, Zhang felt a great blow from the side that sent him sprawling to the ground. His pistol flew out of his hand. Looking up, Zhang saw Dong standing over him. 'He will surely kill me now!' he thought, and tried to crawl away.

But Dong lifted him up and stood him on his feet. 'People practising kung fu should follow the ethics of kung fu,' Dong said sternly. 'You just tried to kill me by surprise! That is not the way of kung fu.'

Zhang couldn't believe his ears. Here was a man he had just tried to kill, and now he was lecturing him on correct behaviour!

Dong saw Zhang's look of surprise. 'Because you also practise kung fu, I do not want to kill you. However,' he warned, 'the next time you try to harm me, I will punish you.'

By this time, Dong's disciples had heard the sound of the gunshot and arrived to check on their master. They scolded Zhang and said that he brought shame on all those who practised kung fu. Embarrassed by his behaviour, Zhang knelt on the ground and cried. He bowed before Dong and declared, 'I am guilty of doing wrong against you. Yet from now on, I promise to be honest and upright. Master Dong, please accept me as your disciple.'

Dong walked over to Zhang and pulled him to his

feet. 'It is always good to correct your mistakes, that is the kung fu way,' he said. 'But you are only a few years younger than me, so I cannot be your master. Let's agree to be brothers instead.' With these words, he and Zhang bowed to each other.

Dong Haichuan became famous throughout the land for his martial art skills as well as his honourable ways. Today, his style of kung fu is still popular in China, and if you wander around the grounds of the Heavenly Temple in Beijing, you may see some people walking around in a circle, practising Dong Haichuan's 'Eight Diagram Boxing'.